# Not Complicated
## A Coffee and Donuts Book

Amanda Hamm

ISBN: 978-0-985065-99-7

*Not Complicated* is a work of fiction. All names, characters, places, events, etc.
are products of the author's imagination or are used fictitiously.

Also by Amanda Hamm

---

A Perfectly Good Man (Coffee and Donuts #3)

Sofie Waits (Coffee and Donuts #2)

Said and Unsaid (Coffee and Donuts #1)


Hearts on the Window (Stories From Hartford #0.5)

The Christmas Project (Stories From Hartford #4)

Collecting Zebras (Stories From Hartford #3)

Jealousy & Yams (Stories From Hartford #2)

Andrew's Key (Stories From Hartford #1)


The 4th Floor Lounge


Meet Cute: 5 Romantic Short Stories


Weathering Evan

# 1

Emmet climbed onto my lap as soon as he finished his donut. It wasn't the sticky fingers on my skirt that made me nervous. It was the fact that he'd only recently mastered the potty.

"Molly," he said. "Molly, I found you!"

I used my napkin to clean some of the frosting from his fingers. "I didn't know I was missing."

"I *found* you," he said again.

It seemed that Emmet only wanted to steal some of my attention from the girls, who were recounting an imaginary adventure for me and Daniel. I directed Emmet's attention to the bracelets on my wrist and let him spin them while I continued to listen.

"Then three dark ninjas jumped out from behind a tree," Brooke said.

"Three?" Daniel raised his eyebrows at her. "From behind the same tree?"

"It was a big tree," Brooke said.

Piper nodded. "Like the one at the castle playground."

"Oh." Daniel smiled his understanding as his eyes slid to the side to include me in his amusement.

"Piper distracted them with a confusion spell." Brooke's arms waved in circles over her head to demonstrate, I believe, what a confusion spell looked like. "That gave me time to take out the first one. Then Piper tied the hands and feet of the second ninja with her magic rope and just as I began a sword fight with the last one, a troll came crashing... wait." She turned to Piper. "It was a troll, right?"

"A thirty-foot troll," Piper confirmed.

"Right." Brooke paused dramatically as she looked between me and Daniel. "A thirty-foot troll arrived on the scene. Piper and I each attacked a leg and we were able to knock it down right on top of the three dark ninjas and once again the Braid Defenders were victorious." She turned back to Piper with her hands up.

Piper placed her palms against her friend's and they moved their hands side to side, then up and down, then performed a series of double and single slaps. Their victory dance looked like the most complicated secret handshake ever. I think they spent as much time working on that as they did the adventures that preceded it.

Daniel and I shared another smile at their antics. He enjoyed the fantasy, and it warmed my heart and my face to see it.

Maddie cleared her throat. "Good story, girls. If you're done with your donut though, Piper, we need to get going."

Piper threw the last bite of donut into her mouth at her mother's words and chewed quickly before she grabbed some water to wash it down.

"See you soon," Maddie said to me at the same time she nodded at Daniel and held her hand out to Emmet.

The little blond boy scrambled off my lap. One of the bracelets he'd been playing with snagged on a button on the front of his shirt and was pulled to the floor during his dismount. It was a silver bangle, and it rolled just enough that I had to get out of my chair to fetch it from under the table.

"Sorry about that," Maddie said.

"No problem." I slipped the bracelet back onto my wrist and remained standing as the Young family gathered themselves to leave the church hall. Maddie directed Emmet to a trash can and her husband, Stephen, waited for Piper.

Piper and Brooke stood and faced each other. They pulled their braided pigtails in front of their shoulders before they placed their hands on their hips and bowed deeply. Two blond braids hung in front of Piper and two brown ones in front of Brooke. Their serious expressions dissolved into giggles as Piper departed.

"Bye, Molly," she said. "Bye, Mr. Devora."

"See you tomorrow," I said with a wave.

Daniel said, "Keep defending the braids."

Piper turned quickly to hide her laugh. I knew Brooke would not be as amused. Sure enough, she was giving Daniel an expression that bordered on pity. "The Braid Defenders do not defend braids, Dad. We have braids and we defend."

"That sounds familiar." Daniel appeared to be searching his memory. "Have you explained that to me before?"

"About a hundred times." She bore her eyes into him, daring him to laugh.

Daniel stared back, scrunching his nose as he dared her not to laugh.

Brooke had the same slightly droopy eyes as her dad, the same wide mouth and the same tiny dimples that flashed as she began to lose the battle. Then she turned to me as though it never happened. "Piper and I want to do fishtail braids for soccer this week," she said. "Can you do that?"

"Fishtail braids?" I looked at Daniel for help.

"Don't worry," he said. "It's much easier than that loopy twisty thing we tried a few weeks ago. I'll send you a link to the video I learned from."

"All right. I guess I still have a few days to figure it out."

"You have forever," Brooke said. She slumped against her arm on the table. "Why do I have to wait until Thursday to see Piper again?"

"I bet you wish you were still in school so you could see her every day."

"Don't even say that, Dad."

"You like school."

"Yeah, but what if we're not in the same class for 4th grade?" Brooke said. "I don't want to think about that."

"Then we'll just have to think of ways to get the Braid Defenders together outside of school."

Brooke perked up a little.

"Molly will help," Daniel said, looking to me for confirmation.

"Of course. I think soccer was my idea for the summer, wasn't it?"

"And it's great." She smiled. "But I still think Dad should have been the coach."

"You are both very lucky that I'm not." He threw me a look and a gentle elbow to the ribs, both of which made me laugh.

When we signed the girls up for soccer, Daniel had been drafted to coach. He had threatened to make me pay dearly for the idea. Another girl joined the team at the second practice and her mom was excited about coaching. Daniel happily handed the reins to her, letting me off the hook as well as himself.

"Sorry to interrupt. My group has broken up."

"Hi, Mom," I said to the woman who had just walked up beside me.

"Linda." Daniel nodded at her. "How are you today?"

"Not bad, thank you."

"You look good," he said. "I like the earrings."

"Thank you again." Mom fingered the white beads hanging from her ears. They matched her smooth blouse and the stripes on her skirt. The outfit showed off her slim figure. It wasn't nice for a 53-year-old mother of three, but simply nice. I hoped I had some of those genes.

"We don't have to rush off if you're still talking," she said to me.

"Um..." I felt as though I'd just sat down, but past my mom I could see that most of the people who'd stopped after church for coffee or donuts had already left. "I guess I'm ready."

"We'll walk out with you." Daniel jumped up and waved his hand at the table to indicate to Brooke that she should clear her place.

Mom asked Brooke about soccer on the way to the parking lot, and she proudly recounted how she had scored her first goal in the last match. We said our farewells as we headed to different cars.

"I will see you both on Thursday," I said. "And it will only *feel* like forever."

Though I was teasing, Brooke sighed her agreement.

Daniel only half-smiled at her reaction and my breath caught for a moment at the idea that he might be thinking the same thing. Then I reminded myself that I didn't want him to miss me. Not like that.

I tried not to look over my shoulder, or think that I might be missing anyone, as I walked to my mom's car. My seatbelt clicked just before she started the ignition. Instead of backing the car from its space, she turned to face me.

"All right," she said. "I've waited much longer than a nosy mother can be expected to wait. It's time to ask what's going on with you and Daniel Devora."

"There's nothing going on, Mom."

"You like him."

"We're friends. Of course I like him." I thought that twenty-four was probably old enough to admit I liked a guy without worrying that anyone would insist I liked him liked him.

"Come on, Molly. Admit you like him like him."

Okay. I was wrong. "Mom, I can't believe you just said that."

"Would you rather I accused you of thinking he's a stud muffin?"

"Oh, my goodness, no," I groaned. "That is not better."

"I wouldn't blame you for thinking that."

"Mo-om." I revived my petulant teenager voice for the one word because she deserved it. Then I resumed what I hoped could be an adult conversation. "I can admit that Daniel is a good-looking guy and that he's nice and funny and... and that he'd be a great catch for *somebody*. But he's not the right guy for me so nothing is going to happen."

Mom nodded thoughtfully and shifted into reverse. She was quiet as she pulled out onto the street, and I hoped that meant she was coming up with a new topic.

"Does Daniel know that?" she asked.

I asked myself if I should just tell her or deflect. I decided on both. "Yes. Why do you ask?"

"Are you sure?" she said. "Because when you were bent over to get that bracelet, he was checking out your rear end."

"Mom! Were you spying on us or something?" We needed to focus on the inappropriateness of her noticing something like that and not what she actually noticed. Because if she was right, it didn't mean anything.

"I just happened to glance over there." She smiled guiltily to say she knew she wasn't fooling me. "But that's not the only time that… Does he know that you think nothing's going to happen?"

"Yes, Mom. If you must know, he did ask me out. Several months ago now. It was just after Christmas. And I told him I didn't think it was a good idea. So everything is clear between us. Clear and simple."

Mom didn't respond right away. I could tell she was trying to be cautious with her words. "Several months might have given him time to hope you've changed your mind," she said, slowly. "Sometimes you… just be sure you're not toying with him."

"I would never do that!" I couldn't believe she'd suggest such a thing, not when she knew about James. He followed me around for nearly two years in high school. I insisted to everyone that we were just friends. I knew he had other ideas though. I let myself be flattered by that. I flirted with him all the time because I was so flattered by the attention. Eventually, he tried to kiss me. The scene that followed was the most embarrassing of my life, probably of his, too. And the rest of that school year was miserable.

Mom and I had always been close. I told her what happened, even though it meant admitting she'd been right all the times she warned me that things would end badly. But I was not a self-absorbed teenager anymore and Daniel was not James. "How could you say I would toy with someone?"

"I'm only trying to remind you to be careful because I do know how much you don't want to hurt anyone."

"Then you should know I don't need the reminder."

"All right. I just can't help worrying that things are going to get complicated."

Mom didn't have to worry. Complicated was exactly what I was doing my best to avoid. Sometimes the problem with having my mom as my best friend was that she could be a little too… motherly.

# 2

The drive to Creekside Living was fairly quiet, once Mom stopped asking me about Daniel. She liked to park under a big tree in the middle of the lot instead of claiming a closer spot. The bit of shade was nice in the summer, though it wasn't terribly hot that day. A warm breeze blew hair across my face as we walked up to the building.

Mom's hair was longer than mine, but it was held in place by her usual chignon. It was an old-fashioned look that somehow didn't look old-fashioned on her, just polished. Gray hadn't come in streaks for her. Her brown hair was artfully woven with silver strands. I wouldn't mind that gene either.

The front doors were thick wood with large metal handles. They looked heavy but had such smooth hinges that they opened easily. We didn't need to open the doors at all that day. A family with two young boys arrived at the same time. The older boy rushed up to push the handicap assist button, and the doors swung open automatically for all of us. Mom waved at the woman behind the desk as the other family stopped to speak with her.

The ground floor was the independent living section. We took the elevator upstairs. The doors opened to face a familiar beige hallway. The dark blue carpet was moderately more cheerful. My eyes followed the pattern to the second door on the right. It resembled a cable-knit sweater. I couldn't explain why that made it cheerful.

Mom knocked.

Neither of us expected an answer.

After a few seconds, Mom opened the door as she called, "Hello."

I hung back until I heard her asking how he was doing. The scent was always the first thing I noticed in the room. I didn't know what actually caused it, but it made me picture a cleaning crew sucking peppermint and spraying disinfectant on everything.

Mom had brought pictures and trinkets from home, and the quilt on the bed was one she made herself. "It's Sunday," she said, "so Molly is with me today."

"Hi, Dad." I put my hand in his and felt a hint of return pressure, the only sign that he was aware of my presence. Dad was sitting in a faux leather armchair that faced the TV. It was on, but he didn't seem to be paying any attention to the show. He stared quietly at the pattern on his quilt.

Mom flipped off the TV and sat facing him on the end of the bed. I took a seat in a wheelchair in the corner, which always felt weird, like maybe I wasn't allowed to sit in a wheelchair if I didn't need one. It was more comfortable than sitting on the bed though.

"I went out to visit Marie and David this week," Mom said. "They're doing well. Marie hasn't said anything about a baby yet."

"I keep saying it's not a good idea to get your hopes up, Mom."

"I can't help it," she said. "Marie has seemed so tired, good tired, and they shared this conspiratorial look. I can't help hoping."

I nodded understandingly. The truth was she was doing a better job getting my hopes up than I was at keeping hers down. Marie was my sister. She'd been married nearly eight years. She announced a pregnancy near the end of the first year with great fanfare and delight. Two weeks later, she lost the baby and had not spoken of her desire for children since. We respected her privacy and didn't ask questions. Mom found this more difficult than I did.

"I know they still have a crib in the barn so they haven't given up hope either." Mom was talking more to Dad now than to me. "Did I tell you Marie raised the price on her strawberry jam this year and still sold all of it? The garden is gorgeous and the apple trees are looking more promising now, too."

My sister and brother-in-law lived on a farm. They moved there after they lost their minds. The summer before her senior year of high school, Marie met an Amish guy. David was a few years older and staying with distant relatives during his Rumspringa, something I'd never heard of before they met. My understanding was that it was a time for him to check out his options before committing to the Amish church. He and Marie worked together that summer at a place that rented canoes. Apparently, she tipped him into the water on purpose and that caused him to fall madly in love with her.

David went home at the end of the summer, but they exchanged old school paper letters on a regular basis. He decided not to join the church and bought a farm about an hour outside Thompsonville to be closer to Marie. He convinced my sister to join him in a nearly Amish lifestyle. Two years into college, she dropped out and married him. Though he hadn't converted – Mom always said he hadn't converted *yet* – he agreed to raise any children Catholic and she agreed to do it with as little electricity as possible. They were Exhibit A on why I was looking for a nice, uncomplicated relationship.

I began to pay attention to Mom again as I realized she'd moved on to telling Dad about me. "The little girl Molly watches is playing soccer now. She's been practicing with her, and it reminds me of when you coached Molly's team. Remember that? Most of you just wanted to have fun, but there was another dad who tried to take over because the girls weren't winning enough."

"I remember," I said. "I remember working a lot harder after that. I wanted to win to prove to that guy we didn't have to win to have fun." I shook my head. "It made sense when I was seven."

"Soccer wasn't really your thing, was it?"

"Piper is much better than I was," I said. "She loves it when she can get the ball away from me."

Mom smiled. "I think being a nanny has turned out to be your thing."

"I think I got lucky."

She turned to face my dad. "She forgets that her mother had a lot to do with her getting that job."

"I don't forget," I said with a laugh. "Thanks for interfering, Mom."

"You're welcome." She talked to Dad about her job at the library before it was time to take him to lunch. I got out of the wheelchair and moved it closer to him.

"We need to get you something to eat now, dear." Mom held his arm and firmly pulled him towards the chair.

He stood in response to the tugging and let himself be guided to a new seat. My dad was about five foot eight. I wanted to be tall when I was a kid and about 6th or 7th grade I'd started measuring myself against my dad. I'd topped out barely half an inch below his height. We'd playfully argued about whether or not I'd reached it for at least a year. Now, his stooped posture made him a few inches shorter than me, and it made me sad to think of wanting to be taller than him.

I held the chair steady as he lowered himself into it even though I'd set the brake. I looked away from the thinning gray hair as I released that brake and began to push the chair towards the door. Mom continued to do most of the talking as we made our way back to the elevator and to the dining room.

"Oh, look," Mom said, "scrambled eggs for lunch today. You'll like that."

I pushed the chair up to a table and Mom brought the food. We sat on either side of him and Mom pulled his hand out of his lap and wrapped it around a fork. He took a small bite of eggs before he set it down again. Mom chatted cheerfully with an older woman who sat with us. After a minute or two, she pressed the fork into Dad's hand and encouraged him to take another bite. She repeated the process a few more times until he would no longer hold the fork.

My parents had seemed more or less the same age when I was little. As I watched them together now, I wondered at how the eleven-year gap had grown to a giant chasm.

****

Both cars were in the driveway when I arrived at the Youngs' house Monday morning. It was unusual for Stephen to be home at that time. Most days he was in town he went to his office early, and got home before Maddie to relieve me in the evenings.

I had a key to the house. I let myself in and knocked at the same time. What started as a compromise was now a habit. Maddie had insisted in the beginning that it was easier for everyone if I let myself in. I understood her point about not wanting to answer the door every morning. I couldn't squelch the feeling that it was wrong to enter someone else's house without in-the-moment permission. I settled on announcing my arrival with a knock. That gave them a chance to stop me on the off chance that anyone was naked. Fortunately for all of us, Emmet was the only one who'd ever been naked.

He was sitting at the kitchen table, fully clothed, eating a bowl of dry cereal.

"Morning, Emmet," I said, nodding to greet his mom at the same time.

He put another handful of cereal into his mouth rather than acknowledge me.

"Good morning, Molly." Maddie handed her toddler a spoon. "Use the spoon," she said. "Piper, Molly's here. Come have some breakfast."

Piper emerged from the next room holding a book. She smiled at me but didn't say anything as she picked up a box of cereal to fill the waiting bowl. I poured some milk into it for her and Emmet held up his cup for more.

Stephen came in tying a tie as I recapped the milk. "Here's a surprise," I said.

He wrinkled his eyes at me in confusion.

"I mean you're usually gone before I get here."

"Oh, right. My flight's not until ten today, but I am on my way out the door."

"Back on Thursday, right?"

He nodded at me as Piper perked up.

"In time to come to my soccer practice?" she asked hopefully.

"'Fraid not, honey. Molly will take you as usual."

She looked at her cereal and mumbled, "Brooke's dad *always* comes to soccer practice."

Stephen sighed. "I know it's not fair, honey. But we do have the concert on Friday."

"Oh, yeah!" Piper wiggled a little dance in her chair. "The Braid Defenders are going to a concert."

"With their dads," Stephen added.

Piper continued to chair dance and hum a made-up tune. She'd been excited about the concert for weeks.

Stephen picked up a suitcase and gave goodbye kisses around the room. Except for me. The nanny obviously did not get a kiss. I got the third, "Be good for Molly," which made me and the kids laugh.

Maddie walked her husband to the door for a private farewell before she went upstairs to finish getting ready for work.

"More cereal, Emmet?" I asked.

He looked at his bowl thoughtfully, then he shook his head and tried to run off. I wrestled him to the sink to clean off his sticky hands.

He held up his hands to me. "No more crumbs."

"I don't know," I waved the washcloth at him threateningly, "there might be crumbs on your face."

Emmet said, "There's no crumbs," but I could hardly understand him through the giggles.

I gently clobbered his face with the washcloth, more because I knew he liked it than because he was terribly messy. Then he ran to the playroom. I watched him pick up a book and begin to assemble a stack. It would only be a matter of minutes before he was insisting I read all of them.

"Maybe we should go to the library this afternoon," I said to Piper. Emmet could use some new material, even if he didn't know it.

"Can Brooke meet us there?"

"It's Monday."

"Oh, right. I forgot." She only looked disappointed for a moment. "We can still go."

Other than planning around a few meetings, Daniel was able to put in his forty hours whenever it was convenient for him. He chose to frontload his workweek with at least twelve hours every Monday. Brooke spent that day with her grandmother, who I didn't know well enough to feel comfortable asking for playdates or shared outings. Brooke went to a facility I'd been instructed to call a camp the other weekdays because day care was for babies. The long Mondays were exhausting for Daniel, but he loved having the time later in the week for things like taking Brooke to soccer practice.

Piper had her book sitting next to her on the table, but she hadn't opened it. "Piper," I said, "you do know that your dad would rather go to your soccer practice than go to work, right?"

"Yeah." She slumped a little. "But it's easy to be jealous when Brooke's dad always watches her."

"You have me to watch you."

"I know." She didn't look fully appeased.

"And it's generally not a good idea to compare your life to someone else's. You can almost always find something to be jealous of, even when there are other things you wouldn't like."

Piper swirled her spoon around the mush left in her bowl. "Brooke doesn't have a mom."

"Molly, read books." Emmet staggered into the room under more books than he could carry. One slid off the top before he got to me and he stopped, staring at it while he considered a course of action.

"She doesn't have a little brother either," I said.

Piper snorted. "I'm sure Brooke has never been jealous of me for having a little brother."

"You never know."

She shot me a look that said she was pretty confident that she did know.

"Are we talking about little brothers down here?" Maddie reentered the kitchen swinging her purse over her shoulder.

"Yes, we are," I said.

Emmet had put down the rest of his stack to pick up the dropped book and the whole thing slid sideways. Determined as ever, he began restacking the books.

"I'll help you," Piper said. She dropped her bowl in the sink and gathered the books with Emmet.

"Well, speaking of little brothers," Maddie said to me, "I believe you met mine at the Memorial Day barbeque."

It felt like a leading statement so I nodded for her to continue.

"He wants me to give him your phone number. How do you feel about that?"

On the one hand, I was flattered. It wasn't every day that a guy expressed some interest in me. On the other hand, while I remembered meeting her brother, Tim, I hadn't spent more than a minute or two talking to him so it was hard to tell if *I* was interested.

"You can think about it if you want," Maddie said. "I can ask you again when Daniel's around. Maybe that will spur him into finally making a move."

Oh, that wasn't good. It sounded as though my mom wasn't the only one who thought there should be something going on between me and Daniel. I wanted to nip that idea in the bud. "No, that's okay," I said. "You can go ahead and give Tim my number."

"You sure?"

"Yeah. He seemed nice."

"Okay." Maddie looked thoughtful. "I'm sure a little jealousy will work on Daniel."

So much for nipping anything in the bud. She was so rooted to me and Daniel as an item that she was willing to use her own brother to make it happen? "Daniel and I are just friends," I said. A stab of familiarity made me add, "And he's fine with that, too."

"If you say so," she said. Then she waved to her kids as she made her way to the front door. "You all have fun today."

We had more fun after a trip to the library. As much as I did enjoy rhyming dust bunnies, I could only read about them so many times before I wanted to stick the book under the couch and pretend it was lost.

For some reason, I was still thinking about kid books when I got home. Or maybe I just happened to think about them again. I asked my mom if she'd ever hidden any from me. She laughed and said she didn't think so. Then she tried to recall specific books she'd read a lot, and whether they'd been favorites of mine or of Marie. There was one that put a sour look on her face.  I think she may have been tempted to hide something even if she hadn't gone through with it.

She let me choose the music for the evening.  Dad always liked to have a TV news show on when I was growing up, even when he wasn't watching it.  We'd kept the habit about two weeks after he moved to Creekside.  Then one night, Mom said, "We need something new."

She switched off the TV with an almost scary finality.  I didn't know if it made her sad to think of Dad not listening to it or if she'd just never liked watching the news.  Either way, she'd been working on her collection of classical music ever since.  She said it helped her relax at the end of the day.

I usually read a book or a magazine, or I texted with Daniel. I could do those and still sort of listen to Mom's music.  Daniel liked to look for errors or continuity problems in whatever show he was watching.  He'd text me notes with no context and usually managed to crack me up.  I'd only just gotten comfortable that night when he sent: `He just said, "It's 98 in the shade." Why is he wearing a jacket?`

We had a rating system for his observations.  I gave him two smileys for that one.

He immediately shot back: `What? That deserves at least 3.`

I'd been stingy on purpose and smiled at his reaction.  I sent: `The judge's decision is final.`

Daniel: `Can the judge be bought?`

Me: `How dare you suggest such a thing? Now you only get 1 smiley.`

Daniel: `Guess the decision wasn't final after all.`

Me: `Guess not. Want to try to lose the last one?`

Daniel: `This is me holding my tongue.`

I set the phone down and reopened my book.  I think I'd gotten through a few chapters before I heard from Daniel again.

He sent: `One woman collapses. A moment later a second woman says, "She's dead."`

I felt my forehead wrinkling up as I tried to figure out how someone dying was funny.  I read the text several times in case I missed a word or something. I was about to reply with only a question mark when he sent me the other half.

    `The second woman's character is a nurse. Her last line was, "I know CPR."`

I laughed out loud and my mom wrinkled her forehead much as I had earlier. I explained Daniel's observation while I gave him four smileys and an exclamation point for the effort.

He replied: `That's more like it.`

I kept smiling as I returned to my book. I was hoping to be interrupted again and also wondering what it might be like to watch TV with Daniel, to see the things he analyzed. That would involve spending our evenings together and my mind wasn't allowed to go there. I tried to focus on the music instead. That was a change I could get behind. I'd never liked the news.

# 3

The next day started out completely normal. Stephen was out of town. Only Maddie was home when I arrived, and that was even more normal than the previous morning. The kids were finishing breakfast. Emmet was wearing his favorite shirt, bright yellow with a picture of a huge tarantula on the front. It was not my favorite shirt.

Maddie said goodbye to Emmet with a kiss on top of his head. Then she moved on to Piper, who was engrossed in a maze on the back of a cereal box.

"Someone slept hard last night." She fingered a particularly tangled section of her daughter's hair. "I'm sorry I'm leaving you with some serious brushing, but she's more patient for you any—" Maddie's mouth fell open as she abruptly stopped talking. She slowly moved pieces of Piper's hair around.

"Mom, what are you doing?" Piper reached up and scratched her head as she ducked it away.

"Nothing." Maddie dropped the hair and motioned me to follow her to a corner.

I followed and looked at her expectantly.

"I saw something," Maddie hissed.

"What?"

"Something crawling on my daughter's head. I think she has lice!"

"Lice!?" I winced right along with Maddie. This was definitely not good news.

"I will give you a hundred dollars to deal with it," she said.

It sounded like she was joking, but she did write my paychecks so I wasn't sure how to respond.

She picked up on the uncertainty. "I'm not kidding," she said. "I'm getting the heebie-jeebies just thinking about it so I would love to have you handle it. But I think lice goes above and beyond the normal nanny duties so I will include an extra hundred this week if you will, um…" She pointed towards her daughter as though she was grossed out even saying the word lice.

"Okay," I said, even though I might have been just as grossed out. "What do I do?"

"First make sure I'm right. Then check Emmet to see if they both need to be treated. Then I guess you need to go to the drugstore and follow the instructions on a package."

I nodded and jumped right into checking Piper's hair. Maddie watched from a safe distance. It didn't take long to confirm her diagnosis.

Piper ducked away from me, too. She scratched her head, and it made mine itch all over. "Why is my hair so interesting this morning?" she asked.

"Um…" Maddie looked at me.

I shrugged back. I didn't know if Piper would freak out, but we'd have to tell her eventually. "Do you know what lice is?"

"Kids at school have had it," she said. "They say it makes your head itch. Is that why my head has been so itchy?"

"Why didn't you tell anyone your head was itchy?" Maddie sounded a bit exasperated.

"I did." Piper matched her mother's tone as she looked at her and then at me.

Now that I thought about it, she had complained about itching a couple of times. I'd dismissed it as regular head itching, non-icky-lice head itching. Like I sincerely hoped I was experiencing at the moment.

Maddie's expression hinted at a similar line of thought. "Well, I need to get to work so… good luck." She pointed at me. "You should try to catch Daniel before he leaves for work. If she didn't get it from Brooke, she's almost certainly given it to her."

That seemed a fair assessment. I waved at Maddie and pulled out my phone to text Daniel: Hate to tell you this but Piper has lice. You should check Brooke.

Piper wasn't freaking out at all. She was still figuring out the maze on the cereal box. I cleaned up Emmet and then sat him back down to look through his hair. He hadn't grown very much of it in his two-and-a-half years. The pale, thin locks were easy to sift through, and I didn't see any bugs.

My phone calmly indicated that Daniel had responded.

Daniel, however, did not sound calm. Ahhh!!!!!!! What do we do!?

Me: I don't know. Have you treated lice before?

Daniel: No. Assume we need something to kill it. Meet me at the Walgreens on Frog St?

Me: Be there as soon as I can.

"All right, guys," I said. "We're going to the store." I instructed Piper to find her shoes, then led Emmet to the bathroom in the hope that we wouldn't have to find one at the store.

Daniel and Brooke lived a few blocks closer, and he only had to wrangle one child into the car, one who was old enough not to need a car seat. I assumed he would beat us there. When we walked through the automatic doors, I wasn't scanning the aisles for products but for the people looking at products.

Piper spotted them first. "Brooke!" she said, turning a corner ahead of me and Emmet, who was in my arms.

Daniel was squatting next to Brooke with an adorably helpless expression under a mop of curly brown hair. He was always shaggy but seemed particularly overdue for a trim. He looked up at me. "There's like a million choices."

His exaggeration was more than slight. There were more brands than I expected though. I set Emmet down before I squatted next to Daniel and picked up a box to read its back.

"They all involve a ton of combing," he said. "But some you leave in longer than others and some you use on dry hair and... Do you have *any* idea what we want?"

I shook my head. Emmet handed me another box to read before I finished the first one. "I could ask my mom, but there were probably different options when I was a kid. Do you know anyone who's had to treat lice recently?"

"Oh! Olivia had it last year." Daniel stood and reached for his phone. "I'll call Kim and see if she has advice."

Kim was his sister-in-law. I hoped she would be helpful because I wasn't getting anywhere. I was trying to read the label on one box while Emmet giggled and put boxes in my other hand as fast as I could get them back on the shelf.

"Hey, Kim," I heard Daniel say. "I'm in trouble. Brooke has lice, and I don't know what to do." He uttered a string of okays and yeahs as she seemed to rattle off a ton of information. I was distracted by Emmet's game and didn't realize Daniel had returned to that bottom shelf until his arm grazed me on its way to grab something from the shelf.

The sudden nearness knocked me off balance. Emmet thought that was funny and tried to climb into my lap. I hoped Daniel thought the toddler was the reason I was now sitting on the floor of a Walgreens, if he even noticed. The girls were looking at humidifiers on the shelf behind us, discussing rather seriously whether the bear or the lion was better.

"Would you really want a lion in your bedroom?" Brooke asked.

"A bear is just as scary."

"Then why do people have teddy bears?" Brooke cocked her head as she put a hand on her hip. "Have you ever heard of a teddy lion?"

It might have been the girls' conversation. It may have been Emmet bouncing on my thigh like a piece of playground equipment. And it may have been Daniel saying, "Those bugs don't stand a chance," as he put away his phone. Something put so much unexpected joy into the moment that I burst out laughing. While sitting on the floor of a drugstore.

Daniel held out his hand to help me off the ground. He also looked amused by something. I bet he knew exactly what was funny though. Me, laughing at nothing.

He turned the box in his other hand to face me. "Kim recommends this one. She said it's really slippery and that makes the combing easier. She also said it's extremely messy, but that they all are. Apparently, there was an outbreak at Olivia's preschool and the parents compared war notes afterwards."

"I'm looking forward to this already," I said dryly. "Emmet, see the box Mr. Devora has." I tapped its front. "Can you find one that looks just like it?"

"Yes!" He looked carefully between the box and the shelf several times.

I had thought it would be an easy task for him since we'd just been playing on the bottom shelf. But now that I wasn't down there directing his attention, he was sticking to his eye level one shelf up. If I didn't help him, we'd either be there all day or one of the girls would grab it first and I'd have a frustrated toddler on my hands. "Look a little lower," I prompted.

"I got it!" He proudly handed me the box.

"Can you grab one more?" Daniel said. To me he added, "They both have pretty long hair. I want to be sure we have enough."

"Got it," Emmet said again.

"Thanks, Emmet." Daniel took the box. "How about you follow us back to our house for this... procedure?"

"Oh, no," I said. "I'm sure you don't want us coming back to your house to make a mess."

"I'm sure I do. Kim said we'll have to get the girls to sit still for an hour or so to comb out all the bugs. I'm thinking that's going to be easier on both of us if they're together."

"Please, can we?" Piper said. "Please, please."

"Please, can we do it together?" Brooke took hold of Piper's hand as she pleaded with me.

"We're talking about a lice treatment here, girls. A messy lice treatment," I said. "Not a party."

"No, we're talking about a battle." Daniel winked at his daughter. "Braid Defenders versus tiny little bugs."

"Yea!" The girls held their linked hands in the air as they cheered.

I had never felt so happy about being completely outvoted. "All right." I motioned everyone towards the front of the store to pay for our weapons.

"I don't believe we finally have something to defend the braids against," Daniel said as he let me pay first.

I laughed.

Brooke didn't. "The Braid Defenders do not defend braids, Dad."

"This time they really do," he said.

She shook her head sadly as though he just was never going to get it.

As we were leaving, I caught sight of the cashier madly scratching her head. It seemed the idea of lice was far more contagious than the actual bugs.

"See you in a minute," Daniel said as we separated to our respective cars.

It was more than a minute, but probably not more than five. Brooke and Daniel lived very close. I had been to the house many times. I had only been there for pickups or drop-offs though. Arriving with the intention to stay for a while felt different. There was an eagerness mixed with the strange feeling that I was about to get caught with my hand in the cookie jar.

Brooke and Daniel waited for us in the driveway and led us in through the garage, which I'd never been inside. Daniel made me comfortable by saying I could drop the diaper bag anywhere. I briefly reflected on how nice it was that I wasn't actually carrying diapers in it anymore. I put Emmet down as well, and he immediately ran across the room to press his face against the back door. We were in an open kitchen and family area. A large, fenced backyard was on display through a wall of windows and the glass sliding door Emmet found.

"All right, girls," Daniel said. "Have a seat while we work out a battle plan."

Brooke and Piper climbed onto stools while Daniel stood at the kitchen island and laid out the contents of the box he'd just purchased. The centerpiece was a bottle of something slippery, messy and likely toxic. There was also a plastic-wrapped comb with teeth so fine I winced at the thought of pulling it through Piper's hair, and a folded paper covered with tiny print.

"Step one," Daniel said, "arm ourselves with knowledge." He unfolded the paper and began to read. "Step two, skip the pictures." He tipped the paper towards me long enough that I knew it had several greatly magnified pictures of lice. Emmet's tarantula shirt was cute by comparison.

"Okay, so we slather this goop," Daniel pointed at the bottle on the counter, "until your heads – and all of the enemy – are drenched with it. We let it sit for ten minutes, then comb forever."

"Forever?" Brooke rolled her eyes at her dad.

"Yes," he said. "Forever. Kim said she had Olivia sit in the bathtub to contain the mess, but Olivia was smaller and I'm not excited about kneeling by the bathtub *forever*."

The girls smiled at each other as he said forever again. He caught me smiling, too. I was happy to let him take charge and amused by the way he acted like he didn't have a clue when I could see the wheels turning. I knew he was trying to be thorough with his planning before he began to implement it.

"I want to go outside," Emmet said.

Daniel nodded. "You read my mind, buddy. I think we're going to attack the lice outside. That way, when we're done, we can just hose you off."

"Yea!" Both girls celebrated and jumped off their stools. Brooke already had her hand on the handle of the back door before Daniel stopped her.

"Wait, wait, wait," he said, giving an exaggerated sigh that got his daughter's attention.

"What?" she asked.

"First... take Piper upstairs and give her one of your swimsuits. You both might want to use the bathroom before you change so we don't have to interrupt anything. Then come back down when you're ready to get wet."

"Okay, Dad." Brooke waved for Piper to follow and they ran off, making as much noise in their excitement as an entire football team might have made on the stairs.

I watched them go. "They think everything is fun when they're together," I observed. I was only thinking out loud and not expecting a response.

Daniel said, "I know."

I turned back to him, wondering if he understood that I meant that for myself, too. This was going to be so much easier with his help. I wanted to thank him for letting me follow his lead, for making it fun for the girls, for being my friend in general. But I didn't want to risk getting mushy or complicated.

Somehow the silence was both. I felt it and prayed that Daniel didn't.

"I want to go outside," Emmet said again. He was tugging on the door handle but not strong enough to open it.

"Hang in there, Emmet," I said. "We're going to go outside in just a minute." I looked at Daniel for instructions... simple, straightforward instructions.

"Here's the plan," he said. "Tell me if you disagree or have a better idea. We take the girls outside, soak their hair with lice shampoo, then pass out some sunscreen while it's soaking in, then we'll get comfortable on the deck chairs for the combing." He glanced at Emmet. "There's a soccer ball out there and an old tiny slide. Will that be enough to keep him busy?"

"I think so. He loves to be outside. He'll probably be happy just looking for rocks."

"Okay. I'll get a stack of towels and a bucket to rinse the comb and..." He looked at the ceiling for a moment and then back at me. "Can we do this?"

"Bring it on," I said

He smiled at me, and as I watched all the hesitation disappear from his eyes I wondered if maybe it was wrong to accept extra money for this.

# 4

We got set up for our lice battle as planned. Emmet kicked the soccer ball a few times, tripped over it, then walked around with a weird bumpy stick like it was some sort of treasure.

Piper and Brooke each sat in a little chair holding a dry washcloth to catch anything they felt running towards their eyes. So far neither of them had used the cloths and that made me feel like we were doing something right. I sat behind Piper and Daniel sat behind Brooke. We started combing near the ends to work out tangles and gradually made our way up to the infestation. When I finally took a swipe near the scalp, I saw two tiny black bugs between the teeth of the comb. I quickly rinsed it in the bucket because I didn't think Piper wanted to see what we were up against.

A minute later, Daniel made his first catch. "Check it out, Brooke." He held the comb in front of her. "One down, who knows how many to go."

"Cool," she said. "I thought they were too little to see."

"Only when they're covered by hair."

"Have you found any, Molly?" Piper asked.

"Don't worry," I assured her, "I'm winning."

"Oh, we should have two buckets," Brooke said. "That way we can see who had more when we're done."

"I meant winning against the bugs, not your dad." I sort of snapped that. I didn't mean to be so harsh, but the idea of counting lice for a contest nearly turned my stomach inside out.

Daniel gave me an understanding wink. "I think we should stay united against the bugs," he said.

I was thinking that I didn't need to feel bad about being paid extra for this after all. I hoped I didn't look as green as I felt.

"Do you think there were lice on the ark?" Piper asked.

There wasn't time to ponder her question before Emmet came rushing towards us. "I need a potty!"

"Okay," I said, even though it wasn't okay. My hands were covered in slime that I tried unsuccessfully to shake off. I sighed at the bucket between me and Daniel and tried to brace myself for the horror of rinsing my hands in water with tiny floating corpses.

I think Daniel must have read my expression well. He said, "I'll take him," as he plunged his hands into the bucket before I could. He swished briefly before he grabbed a towel. He dried his hands while leading Emmet to the back door.

I returned to the unpleasant task at hand, which involved my fingers touching the water every few seconds. It was odd that the idea of sticking my whole hand in was so much worse. I just accepted the relief that I didn't have to and returned to a more interesting question. "What were you saying about lice on the ark?"

"Well, lice are animals, right?" Piper said.

"Yeah."

"If Noah was supposed to get two of each animal, how did he find and carry two of those itty-bitty things?"

"On his head," Brooke said.

"That's entirely possible," I said. "But by the looks of this, there'd have been a lot more than two." I swished another one off the comb and into the bucket. I guessed I was only about a quarter of the way through Piper's hair.

"Doesn't the Bible say there was two of everything?" Piper said.

"Not exactly. They brought extras of some animals so they could eat them."

Brooke peered into the bucket. "Can you imagine eating that!?"

She and Piper tried to outdo each other with disgusted looks and noises before the giggles took over and ended the discussion. They had settled down enough to begin imagining a quest for the Braid Defenders when Daniel and Emmet came back outside. Emmet returned to the place in the ground he'd been poking with his stick. Daniel took his seat next to me.

"Thanks," I said.

"You're welcome." Daniel studied Brooke's hair to determine where he'd left off. As he picked up the comb, he said, "I hope you're not going to try to take advantage now."

"Of what?" I asked.

"Well, there's no telling what you might expect," he cast an oddly tentative glance my way, "now that you know I'm willing to dunk my hands in lice water for you."

"I'd dunk my hands in lice water for you?" I could hardly get the words out through the laugh. "I bet you say that to all the girls."

He shook his head with clearly fake offense. "I can't believe you're laughing at my best line."

I wanted to continue the teasing with a remark about that line being the reason he was currently single. But I felt we were getting a little too close to flirting as it was. I finished a good laugh and focused on combing out yet another section of hair.

Daniel was quiet for a minute, also focused on the job. Then he said, "How about you tell me how you ended up as Piper and Emmet's nanny?"

"That's a really long story."

"I know. I've asked before and you keep saying it's a long story. But we're going to be here for a while." He gestured to the gobs of hair in front of us. "This feels like a good time for a long story. Unless, um…" He pointed more specifically to Piper and I understood he was asking if there was any reason I wouldn't want to tell it in front of her.

I shook my head to say that wasn't a concern. The girls were engrossed in their own story anyway. Daniel encouraged the Braid Defender stories and while they didn't bother me, I didn't need to hear another one. It sounded as though they were facing a robot army this time. The actual battle seemed very much the same as when they fought the ninja and the werewolves and whatever else they came up with. Emmet was now digging up rocks and lining them up on the side of the deck. It probably was an excellent time for me to tell a long story.

"All right," I said. "I, um... I didn't know what sort of job I wanted when I was in college. Since I couldn't think of anything I really wanted to devote my life to, I just wanted to find something I could leave at work. I thought... put in my nine to five somewhere, then come home and think about something more enjoyable. I got a basic business degree thinking I'd be an administrative assistant or something sort of secretarial. I moved back to Thompsonville when I graduated because, well, Dad was getting worse.

"Anyway, right away I got hired at a temp agency. Not as a temp, but at the agency. I helped people looking for jobs fill out forms and do an employment test. The job itself, I liked. But the environment was rather toxic. My boss was in the middle of a divorce, and she talked about it all the time. There was usually just the three of us in the office and the other woman who worked with us was also divorced and extremely bitter. The two of them would get together and it was so ugly. The negativity was stressing me out so I started to look for another job and I'm glad I did because before I left, the first woman's husband – or soon-to-be-ex-husband – started stopping in the office to try to talk to her. Apparently, she wouldn't take his calls and he was pleading with her to keep the trouble between them and stop bad-mouthing him to their kids."

"Oh." Daniel winced. "You definitely needed to get out of there."

"Yeah. I only worked there about six months and it was a looooong six months."

"I'm guessing you weren't looking for a nanny position though?"

I shook my head. "I found a job next at a veterinary clinic, a receptionist position. It started great, but lasted only three weeks."

"What happened?"

"Me and this other guy got called into the manager's office. He said two hundred dollars was missing from the cash drawer, and it had to have been one of us who took it. The other guy immediately pointed a finger, literally, at me."

"What!?" Daniel looked outraged on my behalf. It felt good to know he didn't think I was capable of theft.

"Well, I denied it but didn't go so far as to accuse the other guy because I had no idea what happened. The manager said he didn't know who to believe so either we could both quit quietly or he would involve the police."

"So you left even though you hadn't done anything wrong?"

"I did." I looked down and admitted, "I was scared. I didn't know what had implicated me in the first place so I didn't know if it was something that might also make me look guilty to the police. And beyond that, I didn't want to work for someone who didn't trust me."

"That I can understand." He looked thoughtful and was apparently doing some math. "You've only been out of school two years and I know you've been working for Maddie and Stephen about one of those, plus the six months at the first place. You've got to be getting close to where they come in."

"Hang in there. You're the one who asked for a long story."

"I know. I don't regret it... yet." He smiled just enough for his dimples to tell me the yet was a joke.

I let it go. "How are you doing on the hair over there anyway?" I asked.

"I think I've almost gotten through it all at least once, but I'm trying to be really thorough so I don't have to do it again."

"Me, too. I'm not leaving a pair to repopulate this planet."

"Planet?" His eyes crumpled in confusion.

"That's right. You were inside for most of the discussion about lice on the ark."

"Lice on the ark? I'm sorry I missed that." He laughed and didn't look all that sorry. "What happened after you left the vet's office?"

"I was out of work for a couple of months and getting desperate. I applied at a fast food place and got turned down because she said she knew I'd only work there until something better came along. I couldn't deny that, but neither of us knew how long that might take. It was still sort of demoralizing. Meanwhile," I took a deep breath as I prepared to switch to the other side of the story, "Maddie and Stephen were having a little trouble of their own. They hired a nanny when Piper was a baby. By all accounts, she was a lovely woman who worked for them for more than five years and was great. But she was married, and her husband got offered a big promotion at his job that required a move. The timing was actually not so bad because it was just before Emmet was born. Maddie planned to take two or three months of maternity leave. She was able to stay home and use that time to find a replacement nanny. They hired a woman who seemed nice, but after only three months she moved, too. Maddie didn't mention her reason. The nanny they hired next turned out to be a bad fit. Maddie didn't elaborate, just said there were personality issues."

"She taught me bad words," Piper chimed in.

"Oh," I said. I hadn't realized she was listening. She evidently knew this part of the story better than I did anyway. "So then they hired a woman who was expecting a child of her own. She wanted to be a stay-at-home mom but needed some income. She was expecting a boy who would be fairly close to Emmet's age, and Piper was in school so it seemed like that might work pretty well except for the impending time off she'd need when the baby came. Maddie and Stephen were each going to use a little vacation time and Maddie's mom agreed to help and everything seemed all lined up."

"I didn't like her anyway," Piper said.

"Why not?"

Her shoulder moved up and down in front of me. "She was nice, but… well, I had to go to her house after school instead of her coming to our house."

"Oh, you didn't like going to her house?"

"Yeah. It smelled funny."

"Was it a bad smell?" I asked. "Or just different from your house?"

"Just different I guess."

Daniel's hands slowed in Brooke's hair. "Does our house smell funny, too?"

"Yeah. Yours is worse than hers was." Piper said it in a matter-of-fact tone. "But I still like coming here because of Brooke."

Daniel tipped his head as though he wasn't sure how to take the news. He looked at me. "Is there a problem with the way our house smells?"

"Well…" I intended a bit of teasing, but my hesitation put real concern on his face. "It's fine," I said, firmly. "Everyone's house smells different because of just… a different mix of cleaners and activities and… lives. But your house smells fine. I think Piper is more aware of the differences than most of us. She has a sensitive nose."

Piper nodded seriously, and with pride.

"Me, too," Brooke said.

"Okay, enough about smell," Daniel said. "There was a pregnant nanny, who I think I actually met once, and…"

I filled in the blank for him. "And she had some sort of complications. Her doctor ordered her to spend the last two months of her pregnancy on bed rest. Maddie and Stephen were suddenly looking at a much longer gap to fill. My mom and Maddie's mom know each other from church. They're in the choir together and sit together for coffee and donuts. I guess they were comparing notes at some point. One of them had a daughter in need of a job, the other had a daughter in need of a nanny."

"I see." Daniel nodded slowly. "Everything is starting to come together."

"I talked to Maddie, admitted that I didn't have much experience. I did some babysitting in high school and took a first aid class for that, but hadn't done anything long term. She insisted she wasn't asking me to switch careers or anything, which I thought was funny since my problem was that I didn't *have* a career. She only wanted me to watch the kids for about three months until the other woman could come back. I had just moved back in with my mom, partially due to lack of funds, so I couldn't turn down a job even if it was only temporary and not what I'd been looking for."

"So how did it become permanent?" Daniel asked.

I nodded towards Piper. I didn't know if she saw that or only wanted to explain her part.

"I told my mom and dad that we should keep Molly."

"That's right," I said, even though the phrasing made me sound like a pet. "I was the fourth nanny in a little over a year, and Maddie told me they were reluctant to make yet another change, even if it was back to someone they sort of knew. So when Piper told her she wanted me to stay, she wanted to convince me as well. I felt bad about kind of stealing someone else's job, but I was surprisingly happy as a nanny and didn't have any other options at the time. I had continued to look for work since it was supposed to be temporary, and I got offered a bookkeeping job early on, but they weren't willing to wait for me to finish the nanny gig. Maddie started asking around, and she found someone at her office with a couple of older kids who just needed after school care. The woman who had been Piper and Emmet's nanny before me was willing to take them instead so it ended up working out for just about everyone."

"Especially for us," Piper said. "Molly is the best nanny we've had."

"Wow, thank you." I was truly touched and thought I should explain an earlier comment so she wouldn't misinterpret it. "It's the best job I've had. I said I was surprisingly happy only because I hadn't planned to be a nanny." I turned to Daniel, who still appeared interested. "Remember I said I wanted something I could leave at work. That's the surprising part. I show up at soccer games when I'm off the clock and sit with them – and you and Brooke – after church and it doesn't bother me that the lines are blurred. But I still feel sort of like the job chose me instead of me choosing the job, which is why I say it's a long story and a complicated one at that."

"And why you want to avoid other complications?" The comb slipped from Daniel's hand as he rinsed it in the bucket. He didn't try to fish it out or even look down. He had light brown eyes, some people would say hazel. They told me that he was thinking of what I said when he asked me out. I had admitted that I liked him, too, but that I thought it was a bad idea for us to get involved. If it didn't work out, we'd still have to see each other to get Brooke and Piper together and that could get complicated. He said he understood at the time and nothing had changed. Surely the memory had just popped into his head. It couldn't be something he'd thought about much in the last five months, not nearly as much as I had.

"Hey! Are you guys finally done?" Brooke was turned around to face us, and I realized that I had also stopped working.

"You know what, I think we are." I plunked my comb into the bucket on top of Daniel's. "I've gone through Piper's hair at least twice and haven't found anything for quite a while."

"All right," Daniel said. "Time for phase two."

"What's phase two?" Brooke asked.

He also had Piper's attention.

"One minute." Daniel took the bucket to the fence and dumped its contents into his neighbor's yard. "No one lives there right now," he said, patting the fence, "and now we have a buffer zone." He used the hose to rinse his hands and the inside of the bucket, then he passed the hose to me.

I set it to full pressure before I began to blast my hands. I was going to need a lot of soap.

Daniel had brought out some kids' shampoo. "Hold out your hands, girls." He squirted some into each waiting palm and instructed them to start scrubbing. While the slippery treatment had made it possible to pass the fine comb through long hair, the oily texture did not want to wash out. We passed the shampoo and the hose back and forth, shampooing Brooke's and Piper's hair three times and Daniel's hands and mine at least as many before we started to feel clean. The girls shrieked when we rained cold water on them, but the temp had to have climbed above ninety. I was tempted to splash myself.

Emmet also seemed jealous. Daniel flicked a small spray of water at him before he said, "Do you have a change of clothes for him?"

I did. I took the hose and set it to a mist that I held out for Emmet and the girls to run through while Daniel moved the chairs we'd used back to their usual places. He had retrieved the combs from where he dumped the bucket and stood frowning at them. I guessed he was thinking the same thing I was, that he hoped not to need them again but wasn't sure he should throw them away.

I impulsively turned the hose on him, only for a second before I had it back on the kids. He turned to us with a startled expression. I kept a perfectly straight face and even managed to look a bit puzzled as to how he had gotten damp.

The kids ruined it. They were all laughing and cheering and Brooke yelled, "Get him again!"

Daniel put the combs in his pocket and took a step towards me. The crooked smile was about the clearest dare I'd ever gotten. I doused him one more time. The kids cheered again. The hose was still set pretty fine and his shirt was only speckled with water. He raised his eyebrows. "I don't think you want to start something," he said. "This is my house. I have dry clothes inside. Do you?"

As a matter of fact, I did. I carried a change of clothes for myself ever since I'd had a diaper leak in my lap. Daniel did not need to know that. Perhaps he'd take it easy on me. My outfit was a blue tee and khaki shorts, nothing that would turn transparent on me. And it was really hot and I'd been sitting still for a long time. I totally wanted to start something.

I cranked up the nozzle and sprayed Daniel in the chest. I only had him off guard for a moment before he reached down to grab some hose. He bent it to cut off my supply. Then he walked towards me slowly and purposefully.

All three of the kids were yelling, "Get her! Get her!" The traitors.

"Whose side are you on?" I asked.

They continued to laugh and cheer indiscriminately.

Daniel said, "Just remember you asked for it," before he lunged for the hose.

Knowing that he was stronger, I didn't bother to put up a fight. I dropped it and ran. He chased me around the yard until I was positively drenched, pausing occasionally to squirt whichever child thought it was funniest.

Then Daniel turned off the water and handed out towels. We came inside feeling pretty victorious all around. I noticed that it was nearly noon already. I didn't think we'd been outside for more than an hour. No wonder it had gotten so hot.

The girls ran upstairs to Brooke's room to finish drying and change back into their clothes. Daniel looked at me uncertainly. "Can I at least give you a dry shirt?"

"Let me take care of Emmet," I said, taking him by the hand before he jumped on the furniture in his soggy state. I grabbed the diaper bag and led him to a small bathroom under the stairs. He was capable of dressing himself, but still pretty slow at it. He cooperated in letting me change him so we could be faster. I sent him out and got into my own dry clothes. The shorts were the same. I had four or five pairs of them because they were comfortable and went with everything. I was now wearing a pink shirt though so it was obvious that I changed.

I came out holding a pile of wet clothes. Daniel blinked at me and said, "You cheated." He looked relieved to find out I had cheated.

"Do you have a plastic bag or something I can carry our wet stuff in?"

"Yes." He moved into the kitchen and rummaged through a drawer for a grocery bag. He held it open for me to drop my bundle into.

"Thanks." I took it from him. "For this and for all your help today. I guess I should get Piper and head out."

"It's getting late. Why don't you all stay for lunch?"

"Don't you have to go to work?"

He shook his head. "I went ahead and took the day off. I didn't know how long it would take and I had the time. I do still need to wash her sheets in hot water so it's not exactly playing hooky."

"Oh, yeah. I think we're supposed to wash stuffed animals, too, right?"

"I think so."

"I'm hungry," Emmet announced.

Daniel grinned at the reinforcement. "Lunch?" he offered again.

I didn't need to be asked a third time.

# 5

That stretch of unemployment in my life coincided with Mom making the arrangements to move Dad to Creekside. She made it sound as though I'd be doing her a favor if I came home. She had never lived alone and felt it might add to the stress of the situation. I wasn't sure how much of that was true and how much she only wanted to make me feel better about it. Now that I had some savings again, I sometimes wondered if I should find my own place.

It was complicated though. Mom still acted like she needed me and we both knew Dad didn't have much time left. I had this fear that he was going to die the day after I moved out. If that happened, I'd feel as though I'd abandoned Mom. And while that idea sounded almost noble, I hadn't really liked living by myself either. I wondered how much of the fear came from me needing Mom, too.

Mom and Dad had moved all of us to Thompsonville when I was in elementary school. We lived in a beige split-level house for only a few years before we packed up and moved to a yellow house right down the street. It was the yellow one where Mom and I still lived. I got a phone call as I was passing the beige one.

Mom always nagged me about using the phone while I was driving. I figured if I could see my destination, it didn't count. Besides, it was an unknown number. It would only take me a few seconds to hang up on a sales pitch.

I did not hang up because it was Maddie's brother Tim, the one who'd asked about me. We engaged in some small talk while I pulled into the garage, and I didn't hit my mom's car. I sat on the steps into the house for what quickly became a boring conversation.

He was at a park where he'd met some friends for basketball and called me while they were taking a break. I lost interest as he recounted several of his best plays. When it didn't sound as though he was in a hurry to get back to the game, I reached up to push the garage door button. I hadn't closed it yet because I thought it would be difficult to hear over, but now it had the desired effect of him realizing I'd arrived at home. He asked if I'd be willing to get together sometime and though I agreed, he didn't offer a specific plan before he hung up.

Mom was cleaning up the kitchen when I came in. The white curtains over the sink looked like they had red polka dots, but I knew up close they were ladybugs. Mom was standing under them drying a pan when she turned to me. "Hey, Molly. You hungry?"

"No, I ate with the kids today."

"Good," she said. "I didn't save you any."

"Well, thanks for the hollow offer."

She smiled at my sarcasm. "You know I'd have helped you find something."

I just smiled, too, because I did know that and she knew I was teasing.

Mom reached up to put the pan in a cupboard. "So how was your day?" she asked.

"Far less eventful than yesterday. Though Piper reminded me before I left that I'm supposed to be learning how to do fishtail braids for soccer tomorrow. Can I practice on you tonight?"

"Of course. I think it's funny that you never wanted to braid my hair as a kid and now you've been doing it regularly."

"It's because I didn't do it as a kid that I have to do it now. I figured out I was behind the curve when I had to have a guy show me how to do a French braid."

Mom talked about her day at the library a bit, which was also fairly uneventful, as well as about her visit with Dad over lunch. She asked if I'd be willing to get some groceries the next day, and I took her list. Piper and Emmet usually loved helping me run errands.

We settled on Vivaldi for the evening. Mom turned away from me on the couch and pulled the pins from her hair so I could do my homework. Her hair was even longer than Piper's, nearly to her waist. As I began to brush it, she said, "I noticed you didn't come in right away tonight. Were you on the phone?"

"Yeah, but not while I was driving."

"The last few blocks still count, but I wasn't opening a lecture. I was giving you an opportunity to tell me who you were talking to. Was it Audrey?"

Audrey and Sierra had been my best friends for years. I'd mostly lost touch with Sierra since high school. Audrey and I still talked every few months. "No. It was a guy named Tim James. He's Maddie's brother."

"And why is Maddie's brother calling you?"

"We met at their house on Memorial Day. It sounds like he might be interested in going out with me."

"What about Daniel?"

I sighed so hard I saw my breath ripple Mom's hair. "I'm not dating Daniel so he doesn't have anything to do with it."

"Maybe you should be dating Daniel."

"Do you want me to move to France, Mom?" That's what my brother did. He fell for one of his grad school classmates. She was from France. He married her, moved to France, and hadn't been home since. That was five years ago. They had a toddler that Mom and I had only met through video chats.

"I want my children to be happy," Mom said. "Not everyone has to move to France to make it happen."

"No. Some people just give up civilization." Or they sign up for an age difference that makes them end up feeding their husbands. But I wasn't about to say that one out loud. "I don't want a complicated relationship."

"Okay, Molly. Talk to me seriously. What would be so complicated about you and Daniel? You both speak English."

I separated Mom's hair and pushed half of it over her shoulder so I could focus on one side at a time. "He is nine years older than me. Remember when you thought four years was too much?"

"You're older now. I think you know as well as I do that the difference between sixteen and twenty is bigger than between twenty-four and thirty-three."

I did know. I gave her a hard time anyway. "What would your math teacher say about that?"

"You know I'm right." Mom was sticking to serious.

"He has a child," I said.

"A sweet child that you adore. Sounds more like a bonus than a complication to me."

"But if... I don't know how to be a stepparent."

"No one really knows how to be any kind of parent until they actually are one." Mom turned back to wink at me. "That's why you're lucky to have had older siblings to break us in. But I think you might be more prepared than most."

"What makes you think that?"

"It's not the same of course, but I think being a stepparent would be similar to being a nanny. You're an authority figure to the child – and role model – but certain decisions you defer to the parents."

I hadn't thought about that. I was not ready to let my mom know she was on to anything. "He's a widower," I said. I'd saved my best argument for last.

Mom wasn't impressed. She said only, "So?"

"So I don't want to compete with a memory."

"It wouldn't be a competition. Not if he's ready."

"I don't mean competition exactly, but..." I inhaled sharply, trying to figure out what I meant. "She gave him a child. There has to be some part of him that's still in love with her. That's complicated."

"We all love a lot of people in different ways. I think the love someone feels for a spouse who's no longer living isn't the same as the love you feel for someone who's sharing your life."

I didn't know what to say. It made me sad to think that Mom might have some idea what she was talking about. Though her spouse was still alive, most of Dad's personality lived only in our memories.

Mom spoke into the silence. "Didn't Daniel tell you the ring was only a habit?"

Daniel was still wearing a wedding ring when I met him. It was the previous summer. Brooke had a sleepover with Piper, and Daniel came to drop her off on a Friday before I left. I'd only been the nanny for a few weeks. We chatted for a bit, mostly about how Brooke wanted school to start so she could see Piper more often. I assumed he was married.

I noticed him sitting with the Youngs after church a few Sundays – before I started joining them – with just Brooke. I wondered if his wife belonged to a different church, or maybe no church. I tried to ask Maddie casually by making a bad joke. I asked if Daniel's wife was invisible. When Maddie told me that she had died when Brooke was a baby, I felt like the most insensitive person ever. The only consolation was that at least I hadn't said that to Daniel.

He and I gradually became better acquainted as Brooke and Piper's friendship intensified. One of their 3rd grade classmates had a baking-themed birthday party that he begged me to take both girls to. He was afraid he'd be the only dad and that the women would either assume he was clueless in the kitchen or make a big deal over the fact that he wasn't. I don't know if he would have faced any stereotypes, but he would have been the only guy – other than Emmet and another little brother – and I could see how that might have been uncomfortable regardless.

I'm not sure exactly when I started sitting with the Youngs and Devoras after church. I made a point of saying hello to them each week and that eventually lengthened into the whole coffee and donut time. I'm also not sure when I started thinking of Daniel as a good friend and not just Brooke's dad. At some point we weren't just talking about scheduling and homework. We talked about things we liked and didn't like. I confided in him when my dad stopped talking, about how hard that was.

He told me about the time Brooke came home from preschool and cried because she was supposed to bring her mom to school for Mother's Day and couldn't do it. What Daniel thought might be a deep traumatic scar was a fear of being left out. While all the other kids had living moms, some of them had to work. Daniel's mom wasn't the only grandmother who filled in, and that was enough for the four-year-old Brooke.

Maddie and Stephen had a New Year's Eve party that Daniel and I both attended. Most of the other guests were their work friends so I spent the first part of the night with the kids, which may have been part of their hope when they invited me. I didn't mind. Emmet was in bed at his usual time and while Piper was allowed to stay up, she fell asleep before eleven. I mostly talked to Daniel after that. It was the first time I'd seen him not wearing a ring and felt comfortable asking about the absence.

Sort of. I was a little tense, but I told him I hoped he hadn't lost it. Daniel got this weird look on his face, something between a wince and a smile, as he looked over his shoulder. It gave me the impression that he didn't want anyone else to hear what he was about to say. That made me nervous.

And for good reason. He took a deep breath and said, "I intended to wear the ring until I felt like I had a reason to take it off. But then putting it on was part of my morning routine for so long that I almost forgot I was looking for a reason until I knew I had found one." It wasn't just what he said, but the look in his eyes that made me so nervous I was nearly trembling. Suddenly, the funny guy who gave piggyback rides and invented a meal called elephant puke looked like someone who could get hurt. He looked like someone that I could hurt.

We were interrupted by another partygoer before he could elaborate on the reason he'd mentioned. He found another opportunity about a week later. I went to his house to retrieve Piper from a playdate and the girls were playing a board game they wanted to finish. Daniel said he had enjoyed the New Year's party and asked if I'd be willing to spend more time with him without the kids.

Fortunately, I'd had time to prepare my speech about how awkward that would be if things didn't work out. He accepted my reasoning and assured me we could stay friends. We were going to stay friends no matter what my mom had to say about it.

The trip through my memories distracted me from the braid I was supposed to be practicing. I began to undo it. "This doesn't look right," I said. "And just because Daniel might not have the same aversion to complications that I do, that doesn't make him the one who's right."

"All I know is that yesterday after spending the day squirting Daniel with the hose, you came home a lot more animated than today when you got a call from another guy."

"That means nothing, Mom. If you recall, I came home pretty *animated* that day Emmet went around throwing up on everything."

# 6

I got enough practice that Piper's braids looked like they'd been done by someone who had practiced. We got a parking space on the edge of the soccer field, and she ran ahead while I was still getting Emmet out of his car seat.

Piper quickly found Brooke among the kids and parents on the sideline. As I caught up, I watched the girls briefly examine each other's pigtails before they pulled them forward and bowed deeply. The silly greeting always made me smile.

Daniel was standing nearby. I was somewhat shocked to see that he'd lost most of his hair since the last time I saw him. "That's different," I said, nodding to the top of his head.

"I cut it," Brooke said, a huge grin showing off her pride.

"Really?" I looked between her and Daniel in surprise. I didn't know if it was more unbelievable that he'd let his daughter cut his hair or that she'd actually done a good job. There was still enough to curl slightly on the top, but it was much shorter overall. "It looks good," I said.

Daniel sprouted a mischievous grin. "Are you complimenting her or me?"

"I guess both of you." I pointed at Brooke. "But mostly you."

"Thanks," she said. "He said I might be able to cut it again, but..." She stopped and frowned at her dad.

"But what?" I prompted her.

"Hair grows so slowly. I'm betting he thinks I'll forget before it's long enough." Her expression dared him to deny it.

"What?!" Daniel widened his eyes in feigned innocence. "Where did you get such a crazy idea?"

Brooke plopped a fist on her hip as she took a stance that said she doubted even Emmet believed her dad's act.

Daniel copied her posture. Instead of a serious face though, he smiled down at her and moved his eyebrows slowly up and down.

I had to bite my lip to keep from laughing at the pair of them. Brooke was not amused. She stared back for a few moments before she said, "Come on, Piper," and the two girls ran to join their teammates. The coach had just started lining them up for drills.

I studied Daniel's new look as he watched the girls begin to pass soccer balls back and forth. I wasn't sure what to make of it. He looked older. Not older than he actually was but older than he looked before. It reminded me that he was significantly older than me. That should have been a turnoff, solidifying in my mind the obstacles that kept us safely in the friend zone. It was an attractive haircut though, and the fact that he'd done something a little extreme to please his daughter was even more attractive. Unfortunately, he caught me staring at him.

"What?" he said.

"I... uh..." I touched the back of my hand to my forehead to indicate that if my cheeks were turning pink, it was because it was hot outside. "Forgive me for being shocked that you let a 9-year-old cut your hair."

"She's nine *and a half*," he said with a smile. Then he shrugged. "I usually do it myself, and it's not like I know what I'm doing either."

"Really? You told me that once before. I thought you were kidding."

Daniel playfully narrowed his eyes at me. "Do you ever believe a word I say?" he asked.

"Sometimes." I tried to match his light tone.

He turned to Emmet, who was still sitting on my hip. "Do you know what I did to lose all credibility with Miss Molly Hartigan?"

"Yeah," he said.

"You do?" Daniel smiled at him. "Will you tell me?"

"Yeah."

"Okay. Go ahead."

We both looked at Emmet. The toddler stared back as though he was the one waiting for an answer.

Daniel said, "Was it the time I was late picking up Brooke?"

Emmet nodded and said, "Yeah."

"Even though there was an accident I couldn't get around?"

"Yeah."

"And I called to explain I'd be late. That didn't help?"

"Yeah," Emmet repeated.

"And now Molly will never trust me because of that one strike?"

"Yeah."

Daniel looked at me with a sad shake of his head. "You are one tough critic."

I took a page from Brooke's playbook and refused to laugh. "Do you know that he's two years old and has no clue what you're talking about?"

"And yet *he* believes me," Daniel said. "Emmet, if I told you that I had something for you in my pocket right now, you'd believe me, right?"

"Yeah." Emmet nodded with confidence. Something for him he understood.

Daniel put his hand in the pocket on the front of his shorts and pulled out a tiny car.

Emmet took it happily and then wanted down to play with it.

"I don't know when he left that at our house," Daniel said. "Brooke found it sometime last week, and I keep forgetting to give it back."

A whistle made us pay attention to the soccer practice. Piper was dribbling a ball around a cone and Brooke was attempting to do a cartwheel. The coach began to divide the team for a scrimmage. I checked on Emmet. He was using the front of the car like a shovel, trying to dig a small trench in the grass. Then I glanced at Daniel. He was rubbing the back of his head.

"It feels different, too," he said. "In the interest of full disclosure and earning back some credibility, I'll admit that I evened it up after Brooke went to bed last night. It's short enough that I got out the clippers, which I hadn't used in a long time, so it was more involved than I thought it would be." His eyes floated to his daughter and back to me. "She didn't notice so don't tell her."

"My lips are sealed." I pressed them together. That was a mistake because it drew Daniel's eyes to my mouth. He wasn't thinking what a guy might have been thinking, but it still made me think it. My mind played a brief scene of Daniel leaning forward to kiss me. I directed that thought right out of my head and replaced it with a more practical one. "So Daniel," I said, "you have a decision to make."

"I do?" There was genuine interest in his voice.

"About the concert tomorrow."

"Okay?" The interest appeared to fade.

"Are you not as excited as the girls?"

"I'm sure the concert will be fun. I'm just not excited about the half hour drive there and back with Stephen." Daniel shifted his weight as soon as the words were out of his mouth. "I shouldn't have said that. I don't dislike him. I just..." He looked at me, then glanced at Emmet. The kid was now plucking grass and burying his car in it.

"What's wrong with Stephen? He's nice."

"I didn't say he wasn't." Daniel paused. He clearly had something he didn't really want to say and I waited patiently for him to say it anyway. "He just has this annoying habit of asking me if I've read a certain book or seen a movie or something and when I say no, he proceeds to talk to me about it anyway. And ask questions. We end up having a conversation that involves me saying a lot of things like, 'I can't really judge a special effect based on a description,' or 'I'd need to know how that decision played out,' or something equally awkward that feels like reminding him over and over that I already said I didn't know anything about it."

The frustration in the reenactment made me laugh. "Let me ask you something," I said. "How is that different from you texting me about TV shows I'm not watching?"

Daniel's face showed surprise for only a moment before he recovered and rolled his eyes at me. "I can't believe you're even trying to make that comparison. It's totally different. Do I need to list all the reasons it's different?"

"I think you do."

He made a show of clearing his throat and shifting his weight in preparation, obviously giving himself time to think of reasons. "Reason number one," he said, "I explain the mistakes well enough that you don't need to see them. Number two, you're only expected to rate them, not speak to the accuracy."

"Are you suggesting you make some up?"

Daniel ignored my interruption. "Reason number three, Stephen isn't trying to be funny. Reason number four, I'm a lot funnier than he is anyway."

The boast made me laugh because he was kidding and because that made it true.

"So what's this decision?" Daniel asked.

"Well, it sounds like you might be glad to know that Maddie called me this afternoon and she said Stephen has to stay an extra day. He's taking a flight tomorrow that won't get in until after seven. Rather than make you late, Maddie said she'd give me his ticket. She wants me to work something out with you to either have you take both the girls by yourself or I could take Piper and you… Anyway, I told her I'd make sure Piper can still go. It doesn't make sense for me to drive separately when we'd end up in the same spot. So here's the decision… you can either take Piper and Brooke by yourself or you can let me tag along."

"Do you want to go?"

I shrugged. "It might be fun. I'm not familiar with the band though."

"It would be a shame to let the ticket go to waste."

"Pretty lukewarm response there, mister," I said. "I hope you're not suggesting I have some annoying habit you'd rather not deal with."

Daniel opened his mouth, looking delighted at the opportunity I had deliberately created. I guess he decided to let it pass. He only smiled at me for a moment before he said, "You should come with us."

"Thank you," I said. "I will come. You can pick me and Piper up together and—"

"Molly! Molly, look what I found!" Emmet was holding up a tiny purple flower.

"That's pretty."

"It's for you," he said.

He'd ripped the flower clean off the stem so I held my hand out for him to drop it into. "Thank you."

"Another one!" Emmet reached into the grass and snatched up another purple flower, again minus the stem.

I accepted it the same as the first.

Emmet scanned the grass for more. Daniel found one first. He pulled it up with a stem and presented it to me. "Can I give you one, too?"

I took the teeny tiny flower. Even with the stem, it was easier to let him drop it into my hand with the others. "Thanks," I said, to both of them because Emmet was dropping in another one as well. "I don't know what I'm going to do with all these treasures."

Emmet beamed and continued to hunt for flowers. Daniel's face said he'd picked up on my sarcasm. I ignored it so Emmet would continue to think I loved the flowers. They were making a pretty pile in my hand. I just knew from experience that they would be shriveled and dry within an hour. I squatted to receive more.

Daniel mumbled something above me. I wasn't sure I heard what he said. I didn't ask him to repeat it because it sounded like, "I'd give you real ones if I thought you'd take them."

If that was what he said, I'd have to ask what he meant and I did not want to know. Despite my certainty that I didn't want to know, my brain began to puzzle it out. Flowers were often considered romantic. Did Daniel think that I wouldn't accept flowers because I'd read romantic intentions that weren't there? Or did he want to make that kind of gesture? I didn't want him to want that. Except that maybe I did. There was a part of me that I didn't want to acknowledge that wanted Daniel to want to give me flowers regardless of how positive I was that I didn't want to want that. This was yet another reason I didn't need complications in my life. There were enough of them in my head.

\*\*\*\*

Maddie had invited a few friends from work – she was a lawyer – to come over Friday evening. They weren't expected until after we left for the concert and after Emmet was in bed. I was helping her prepare snacks for her guests while I waited for Daniel to arrive. Emmet was also helping. That's why we weren't finished.

"I think that's enough," I said. "Put it right here." I pointed to the tray in front of Emmet. He was in charge of rolling the truffles in sugar. He kept trying to lick the sugar off his fingers though. That put me in charge of keeping his hands away from his mouth. I'd already helped him wash them three times. The next time, we were going to be done whether there were truffles left to coat or not.

"Have you heard from Tim?" Maddie asked out of the blue.

"Sort of," I said. "I mean, he called me once, but didn't exactly ask me out. We just had a random chat."

"That sounds about right." She pulled a pan from the oven and sighed as she dropped the potholder on the counter. "I shouldn't say anything bad about my brother. He's just... flighty. And that's hard for me to relate to. Do you think you're going to end up going out with him?"

"Take this one, Emmet." I shrugged. "I guess I probably will if he decides to ask."

"If he happens to call tonight, make sure Daniel sees a guy's name on your phone."

While I considered Maddie a friend, she was also my boss. I wasn't sure how much of my love life I wanted to get into with her. I tried to steer the conversation into more hypothetical waters. "Isn't trying to make a guy jealous kind of childish?"

"Oh, yeah. I'm not suggesting you try to date them both or play any relationship games. I'm only talking about you getting Daniel's attention. Something needs to spark you two because you're clearly a perfect match and I cannot believe it's taking this long for you to get together."

This did not feel very hypothetical. Emmet's hand went for his mouth while I was distracted. I grabbed his wrist right as his tongue made contact. "Ugh."

The doorbell rang.

"Saved by the bell," Maddie said. "I'll take him to the sink. You go have fun."

She led Emmet away as Piper called, "I got it!" from the next room.

"Thank you for your help," Maddie said as I left the kitchen.

I waved to her and Emmet before I rounded a corner to see Piper opening the front door. She immediately pulled her braids forward and executed a lovely bow. I assumed, based on the excited giggles coming through the door, that Brooke was mirroring the bow just outside my line of sight.

"You look ready to go," Daniel's voice said. "Is Molly ready?"

"I'm right here." I showed myself to Daniel and Brooke, then reached for a small purse on a hook. I'd already stashed the diaper bag in my car for the evening. "Say goodbye to your mom, Piper."

"Bye, Mom!" she yelled.

"Have fun!" came the response. I think Piper heard it, even though she was already on the porch. I followed her out and locked up behind us.

I was a natural homebody. It surprised me that the nervous energy beginning to course through me as I watched the girls climb into the backseat felt like a good thing. I suppose everyone needs to stretch their comfort zones every now and then, if only to appreciate the borders. I still started the trip a little jumpy. It had been quite some time since I'd ridden in a car with a standard transmission. Each time Daniel reached over to shift, I felt as though he might be reaching for me.

The girls quickly settled into imagination mode. "I was thinking," Brooke said, "that the Braid Defenders might see some action at a concert."

"Like what?" Piper was eager as ever.

"Maybe the vibrations will be so loud that the ceiling will begin to crumble.

"Oh, yeah. I will use my super speed and super strength to grab the pieces as they fall and hurl them out of the way." I could see Piper's arms waving out of the corner of my eye.

"Perfect," Brooke said. "Meanwhile, I'll guide everyone to safety. Do you think we'd need to go backstage?"

It sounded like the Braid Defenders had a good story about saving the day as usual. Though it was more original than most of their supernatural attacks, I decided I'd rather tune them out in favor of some grown-up conversation.

"Piper and I downloaded a couple of songs," I said to Daniel, "and we've been listening to them today in hopes of hearing something familiar tonight."

"You know what they say about great minds?"

We compared notes on which songs we'd now heard. The concert was Brooke's idea. Several months ago she'd started asking Daniel to take her to a concert, a *real* concert. He guessed that she meant something other than a kiddie band. He started keeping his eyes open for something in the area that might be appropriate to go to with a child.

He found a concert with a Christian rock band. They seemed to have mostly upbeat songs, which he thought Brooke would like. And with a Christian band, he figured that even if he didn't particularly enjoy the music, at least it'd be unlikely that he'd feel the need to put his hands over his daughter's ears at any point in the evening.

I'd only been to one other concert, with a guy I dated my first year of college. He was my first boyfriend. Determined to fix the mistakes I'd made with James, I jumped into that relationship with both feet. I told him I loved him when he said it first even though I wasn't sure. We were together almost four months and fairly inseparable. Then I realized that I wanted to be separable. It just wasn't working for me. He seemed to take it all right in the moment, seemed to understand that I was truly sorry we didn't make a good couple.

But then he called me a few days later and begged me to change my mind. I knew I shouldn't. I held my ground through an incredibly sad phone call. And another one the next week. He called me five times altogether after we broke up. I didn't answer the last one. I heard the message about how much he missed me though. I could still hear it if I let myself.

Instead, I thought about the music I'd listened to with my mom the previous night. "Daniel," I said, "are you familiar with the *Thunder and Lightning Polka?*"

"No. Is that a song?"

"Yes," I said. "It's a polka. My mom had it on a loop last night."

"Stuck in your head?" He offered a little sympathy in his tone.

"Exactly. There's a part where the instruments sound happy and it's like you can picture the storm letting up for a while. Am I right?"

"Uh…" I was looking at his profile and saw little creases by the side of his eye. Then he smiled as he realized what I was doing. "Absolutely," he said. "I can tell just by the fact that you describe it as happy that it sounds like light rain."

"Like a pitter-patter break in the thunder. That's how you'd describe it?"

"Exactly. And the strings… there are stringed instruments in this song, right?"

"Yes."

"I believe you'd agree with me that they…" Daniel took a moment to straighten his face. "You agree that they play some notes?"

"They totally do."

"Right." He nodded. "I'm glad we talked about it. Now I've been meaning to ask you… have you read *Take Your Eye Off the Ball?*"

"No," I said. "That's a book?"

"It is. Would you like to guess what it's about?"

"Of course. That's much better than having you tell me. Is it, um… sports related?"

"Yes." Daniel nodded. "Football, which *is* a sport. I like the diagrams that the author uses. Don't you think they're helpful?"

"I can imagine diagrams being helpful."

Daniel sent me a quick sideways look that made me give up on being serious.

Then Brooke piped up from the backseat, "You guys are so weird."

"Thank you, honey," Daniel said.

"Weird is not a compliment, Dad."

Daniel flashed her a smile in the rearview mirror. I glanced back in time to see her roll her eyes at him. Then she turned to slap Piper's waiting hands and finish the victory dance she had apparently interrupted to interrupt us.

There were two bands and I think I actually preferred the opening act, even though we hadn't researched them. We were seated pretty far back in a section that wasn't crowded. The sound was still good. When the headliners played the first song we recognized, both the girls started dancing in the aisle. Daniel pulled me out to join them.

We had so much fun that the girls were talking about it all the way home. They recounted their favorite parts and sang a few lines. I did not try to have a separate conversation with Daniel because I wanted to hear their enthusiasm. When we stopped in front of the Youngs' house, Brooke said, "When can we do this again?"

"I don't know." Daniel put his hand up to stifle a yawn. "If we did it all the time, it wouldn't be special."

"It'd still be fun."

Piper was nodding alongside her friend's assertion.

"I'll keep my eyes open, but I really don't know when another appropriate concert might be an option."

Brooke didn't appear satisfied; neither did she try to argue with a serious answer.

Piper grabbed the door handle to let herself out.

"Keep defending the braids," Daniel told her.

She smiled as she got out, but I could hear Brooke's exasperated sigh.

"Dad," she was saying as I also got out, "we do *not* defend braids."

"Is that so?" Daniel waved at me.

"Thanks for driving," I said as I closed the car door.

I walked Piper up to her house before I took my car home. I was ready for bed and a weekend.

# 7

When I came downstairs Sunday morning, I found my mom lying on the couch with a rag on her forehead. I tiptoed closer to investigate. She appeared to be sleeping so I slipped into the kitchen and tried to get myself some breakfast as quietly as possible.

Mom didn't stir as the time ticked by. I didn't want to wake her. If there was any chance she wasn't too sick for church though, she'd be annoyed at having to get ready in a rush. I stood in front of her deciding what to do. Her eyelids fluttered open and her hand came up weakly. "Stay back," she said, her voice raspy. "I've been throwing up and you don't want to catch it."

I nodded that I understood. "Can I do anything for you before I finish getting ready for church?"

She shook her head slightly and closed her eyes as though the effort pained her.

"Are you sure?" I asked.

Her hand came up and lifted the rag towards me. "Could you maybe rinse this with cold water?"

"Sure." I took the rag, feeling the heat it had absorbed from her head, and carried it to the sink. I rinsed it until it felt cold and squeezed out the excess before I brought it back to Mom.

When I put it on her forehead, she breathed out the word, "Thanks," in a momentarily contented sigh. I knew how she felt because of all the times she'd done the same for me over the years. Her eyes opened again as she said, "Now wash your hands." She was still the mom.

"I will," I assured her.

"And… you're going to visit your father after church, right?"

I said, "Of course, Mom," but I was humbled by the fact that she knew I'd already thought about how much harder that would be without her.

I left her alone to brush my teeth and stayed upstairs until it was time to leave. Our church was called Sacred Heart. It had a traditional design, complete with stained glass windows and big, wooden doors. Mom always needed to be early to prepare with the rest of the choir. I arrived early without her out of habit.

The church was quiet as I took a seat. A few people were whispering in a back corner, and I heard pages rustling in the choir loft. The scene should have felt common, like most Sundays. A sudden unsettled feeling gave me the sensation of being disconnected, as though I was looking at myself in the church from far away. I didn't think it had anything to do with my mom being sick. She was otherwise strong. This flu was an inconvenience and not a threat. I would almost describe the feeling as a paranoia, a sense that something unknown was coming for me.

I tried to shake it off as the choir began a prelude. They sang about resting in the Lord. The lyrics seemed directed at me as I started to pray that God would see me though whatever was coming. Or that he would help me stop feeling as though something was coming. It didn't make any sense.

I didn't fully put the weird feeling out of my mind until the mass was over, when I'd walked into the parish hall and Daniel placed a cup of coffee in my hand. He smiled at the tan liquid, and I knew he was thinking what he thought every week. That my idea of a cup of coffee was more like coffee-flavored milk.

"I'm not going to apologize for liking what I like," I said.

He picked up his own black coffee. "I didn't say anything."

The innocent tone didn't fool me. Piper and Brooke had each picked out a donut and had already claimed places at a table to devour them. Stephen carried two donut plates over and set one down for himself before he pulled out a chair for Emmet to climb into. Maddie, Daniel and I remained standing by the table as his sister-in-law Kim walked up to say hello.

"Good morning," she said. "How are we doing? No sign that the lice are regrouping?"

"I hope not," Daniel said.

Maddie only shuddered.

"I checked Piper a couple of times since Tuesday and haven't spotted anything," I said.

"We got 'em." Daniel gave me a confident nod.

"What about the grownups?" Kim asked. "After we doused Olivia the second time, I went ahead and treated myself even though Brad couldn't find any on me. I thought it was the only way to make my head stop itching."

Daniel shrugged. "I haven't felt anything."

I was less nonchalant, or less concerned with appearing nonchalant, so I admitted the truth. "I made my mom look through my hair very thoroughly Tuesday night."

Kim smiled understandingly.

I noticed that Maddie's fingernails had found her scalp. "Stephen," she said, "you're checking me for lice when we get home."

He'd looked up only at the sound of his name. "Uh..." After a moment to catch up, he said, "Okay."

"You all have a good Sunday," Kim said. She moved away patting her round belly. It appeared her third kid would be arriving soon.

Maddie took a seat next to her husband, still scratching her head. Daniel gestured me to the last chair and turned another one to join our table. The girls were still talking about the concert, but also mentioned that they wished they could have won on Saturday. Their soccer team was now one and three.

Our pastor, Monsignor Loy Mystery, stopped at the table to say he hoped my mom would feel better soon. The man was amazingly on top of things. He'd prayed for me when I couldn't find a job and knew I'd found one before I told him.

Maddie and Stephen took their kids home shortly after he moved to greet the next table. I said I'd see them all the next day. Daniel gave Piper his usual farewell and Brooke gave him her usual response about having braids and not defending them. Father and daughter continued talking and I wasn't listening.

I didn't know I wasn't listening until I looked up from a chip in the table to find a question hanging in the air. Daniel and Brooke were both looking at me. My gaze flickered between them, trying to at least figure out who had asked me something.

"Um… what?" My eyes landed on Brooke. She looked safely inquisitive whereas Daniel's light brown eyes had begun a search that seemed to pierce my surface.

"Why do you like to sit by yourself?"

"I'm sitting with you." I answered slowly. Even knowing the question, I wasn't caught up.

Brooke's eyes squished together. It sort of looked as though she was trying to hold them in place to keep from rolling at me. "We saw you in church this morning. I asked Dad – again – if we could sit with you, but he said you like to sit by yourself. Why?"

All that work to get to a question, and I still didn't know how to answer it. Daniel had asked me once if I'd mind company in the pew. He immediately rescinded the offer, saying to forget he asked. He was apparently able to read my discomfort before I could express it. What I didn't express was that I *didn't* want to sit by myself. Church felt like a family thing and my family had abandoned me one by one. Mom joined the choir when I was still a kid. Marie switched her membership to a church closer to the farm while I was in high school. Matthew was still there when I came home my first summer of college. Then he left me and Dad when he joined a church in France.

Dad was the only one who hadn't left me by choice. If I thought about that too much, I'd start to blame God for taking him away from me. That wasn't a thought I wanted to have any time, let alone while trying to praise him. I would love to sit with Daniel and Brooke on Sunday mornings, but that idea scared me. What if I started to wish they were my family?

I didn't know how much of that – if any – Daniel had sensed. Maybe he really thought I preferred to sit alone. How could I possibly explain to Brooke that I'd like her to sit with me without actually inviting her to do so?

She must have gotten tired of waiting for my answer. "Is it because you always have?" she asked. "That's why Grandma said she goes to church on Saturdays. 'Cause she always has."

"I *am* a creature of habit."

A cough came from my right. I recognized that Daniel was covering a laugh because he recognized a dodge even if his daughter didn't. Brooke offered me the way out though. It would have been rude not to take it.

"Dad says that all the time," she said. "Why would anyone call themselves a creature? That's like a monster, right?"

"I am so going to start saying I'm a monster of habit," Daniel said. "That is much cooler." He smiled at both of us.

I appreciated it and returned the smile.

Brooke's shoulders sagged and her head began to shake. "Dad," she said, "that is not cool."

"Sure it is. We always read before bed because we are *monsters* of habit."

"Dad." Her tone was a fascinating mix of pity and warning. It seemed to imply he should be careful because someone might actually die of boredom if he ever said that again.

"What?" Daniel said innocently.

"Dad."

"What?"

Brooke blinked as though she'd lost track of the conversation. "What what?" she asked.

"You keep saying my name," he said. "Aren't you trying to get my attention?"

She exhaled slowly, clearly annoyed with herself for letting him get the upper hand. Then her dimples popped in for a fraction of a second. "Dad is not your name," she said simply.

"It is to you."

"Well, I'm done." She picked up her empty paper plate. "Can I go to the bathroom?"

"Sure. We'll meet you by the front door." Daniel grabbed my trash as well as his.

"Thanks." I followed him to the door and waited with him for Brooke.

He tipped his head to examine me. "Molly, are you okay?"

"I'm fine."

"Do you think you might be coming down with what your mom has?"

"No," I said. "What makes you think I'm sick?"

"You just… seem a little off today."

At the moment, it had to do with where I was headed next. Visiting my dad was getting more and more challenging the less he responded to it. When he first stopped talking, he could still play cards. It was strange that he could follow the rules of Gin even though he couldn't tell me my name. It gave us something to do though, a way to pass time with him and feel as though he noticed. "I feel awful for admitting this, but I'm worried about visiting my dad on my own. My mom usually does most of the talking."

"Would it be easier with company?"

Was Daniel offering to come with me? The generous offer was unexpected to say the least.

"Brooke and I could meet you there. Unless it would be weird with people he doesn't know."

"I…" I didn't want to say that he no longer knew anyone. "Thank you," I said. "That would be great if you're sure you don't mind."

Brooke bounded out of the bathroom and Daniel turned to her. "Change of plans, honey. We're going with Molly to visit her dad today."

"All right." Brooke sounded fairly indifferent and may have only agreed because she knew she had no choice in the matter.

"I'll follow you," Daniel said as we entered the parking lot.

I went to my car and made sure I saw Daniel's behind me before I turned onto the street. I parked under the big tree in the middle of the Creekside lot. I liked it as much as my mom did. I was her daughter through and through, and there was no point fighting it.

Daniel parked right next to me and we walked towards the large, daunting building in silence. Until Brooke noticed the silver squares by the doors and said, "Can I push the button?"

I nodded at her. She punched it and jumped forward just enough to need to jump back as the doors swung open. Cooler air swept towards us to usher us inside. The desk clerk tipped her head to me as I led my guests past her to the elevator. We rode up to the second floor. I knocked on my dad's door. The lack of response was expected, but I hesitated.

I leaned closer to Daniel and whispered, "When we came a few weeks ago, he wasn't wearing pants. I should probably go in first."

He turned to his daughter and said, "Molly's just going to make sure he's home first."

I turned the knob slowly and called, "Hello," as I entered. Dad was dressed and sitting in his usual chair. I motioned Daniel and Brooke in after me. "Hi, Dad." I took his hand and felt that twinge of greeting. "I'm afraid Mom is sick today. Nothing serious, just a stomach bug, but she had to stay home. She wouldn't want you to catch it from her. I brought some friends today though. This is Daniel Devora and his daughter Brooke."

Daniel said, "Hello, Mr. Hartigan."

My dad kept looking at his hands.

Brooke stared at him for a minute before she backed towards the corner and sat herself in the wheelchair.

I gestured to the end of the bed. Daniel sat, and I sat next to him.

"It looks as though Molly and Linda have tried to make you comfortable here," Daniel said. "Lots of things from home." He waved a hand towards some family photos on the wall and a crucifix that used to belong to my dad's parents.

"Mostly my mom," I said. "She made this blanket herself." I patted the space on the bed between me and Daniel.

"I suppose one advantage to a place like this is not having to cook. Molly told me you mostly like the food. Is that right?"

"He specifically mentioned being a fan of the lasagna. Said it was *almost* as good as Mom's."

Daniel nodded. "Did Linda make it to see you before she got sick yesterday?"

"She was here in the morning," I said. "She knew you'd want the news from Marie, right, Dad? My sister is expecting a baby in December."

"Hey! That is good news." Daniel turned to congratulate me with his eyes on the coming niece or nephew. Then he returned his attention to my dad. "Another grandchild. That's a big deal."

Dad didn't give any indication that he knew what we were talking about. My throat tightened with the thought that he wouldn't be here to welcome the baby anyway.

Our visit continued the way it started. Daniel tried to talk about something, and I awkwardly answered for my dad. Brooke entertained herself by pushing the wheelchair forward and back in the limited space she had.

We didn't stay for lunch. One of the staff would assist Dad if family wasn't there. As we walked out, I wondered what Brooke thought of the experience. It was possible she was still deciding what to make of it.

She looked up at me and said, "Molly, why is your dad so old?"

"Well, I'm older than you are so it should make sense that my dad is older than your dad."

"I guess."

"He also… he has a disease that makes him seem older than he really is."

Brooke nodded slowly, still looking unconvinced.

"Plus, I'm the baby of my family," I said. "My dad wasn't quite so old when my brother and sister were my age."

A sudden smile lit Brooke's face. "I'm going to have siblings," she said. "Dad promised."

"Whoa!" Daniel stopped walking and turned to his daughter. "That's not what I said."

"You said you wanted to have more kids."

"I did say that I would like that, but I think you're old enough to understand that we can't always have what we want."

"Yeah, I know." She sullenly kicked at a rock as we started walking again.

"Okay," Daniel said. "It's important that you know I wouldn't promise something I might not have control over. Even if we are lucky enough to expand our family, it's not going to happen anytime soon."

"I know." Brooke sighed. "Babies take forever to grow. And first you have to get married." She turned a big grin in my direction.

I think the bottom fell right out of my heart. It was one thing for meddling adults like my mom to think there was something going on between me and Daniel. It was something different for an innocent child to believe it. If Brooke expected me to marry her dad, she might actually get hurt. What was I doing letting them join me on this emotional visit?

I was going to have to make some changes. Starting immediately. Playdates would be strictly playdates. I would return to sitting with my mom after church. At the soccer games...

The more I thought about it, the more I realized how much of my life had gotten tangled up with Daniel's. To an outsider, it could look as though I was deliberately trying to spend time with him. It looked like that to me, too. Even if I thought Daniel and I were clear about the nature of our relationship, I needed to back off fast before wires got crossed. I'd already hurt too many people. Daniel and Brooke were not safe around me.

# 8

Mom missed work on Monday, but I did not. So far I had managed to avoid getting sick. I unlocked the front door to the Youngs' house and rapped my other hand against it as I opened it.

The kids were having breakfast and Maddie was reading something on her phone, or staring at it. She looked up as I entered the kitchen. Before she could open her mouth, Piper said, "Molly's here. Now ask her."

"I was about to," Maddie said. "Piper thinks she needs to see Brooke before Thursday. She wants you to pick her up early from day care like you did a few weeks ago. You're welcome to say no if you don't want to watch another kid and of course Daniel needs to give his consent."

"I see," I said. "This feels like a lot of plotting for first thing Monday morning."

Maddie nodded as she stood up. "Go ahead and think about it. I'm fine with whatever you and Daniel want to arrange. Or not." She dropped the phone into her purse and started up the stairs.

"Please, Molly." Piper was giving me some serious puppy dog eyes.

Most of the time, my job was actually easier when Brooke was around. The age difference between Piper and Emmet meant that they usually liked to do different things. With Brooke to entertain Piper, she didn't care if I spent more time with Emmet. But I didn't want to look like a pushover. "Well, you know she can't come today," I said. "And you're going to have practice together in only three days."

"Three days is a long time." Piper wasn't pouting. She was simply stating what seemed to her to be an irrefutable argument.

"Milk!" Emmet held his cup towards me.

I uncapped the jug of milk and held it ready to pour. "Set your cup down."

The plastic bottom tapped hard against the table.

"Now how do you ask nicely?"

"Milk, please."

I smiled and filled his cup.

"Molly?" Piper said. She looked at me expectantly. "Will you please call Brooke's dad if I put away the dishes extra fast?"

"All right. Don't break anything."

She jumped up to open the dishwasher and begin her chore. I heard her mumbling under her breath about how everyone *knew* not to break the dishes. I got Emmet cleaned up and Maddie left for work before I sent Daniel a text asking him to call me if he was willing to let Brooke come over later in the week.

I was sitting on the couch going through a stack of books with Emmet when I got a call. "Oh, look," I said to Piper, "it's your social secretary."

She wrinkled her eyes at me as though she had no idea what I was talking about. She probably didn't so I guess it was a bad joke. I said, "Never mind," and answered the phone.

"What kind of playdate are we talking about?" Daniel said right away.

"Piper wants to know if I can pick Brooke up early from day, uh… camp again sometime this week. How do you feel about letting her spend an afternoon here?"

"It's just as easy for me to pick her up there as at camp. You sure it isn't too much trouble for you?"

"I don't mind."

"What day?"

Piper was sitting on the floor in front of me reading her own book. I tapped the carpet next to her with my shoe to get her attention. "What day do you want Brooke to come over?"

"Tomorrow."

She said it so loudly I knew Daniel heard her. I said, "It looks like she needs to think about it for a minute."

Daniel laughed and Piper said, "Tomorrow!" even louder.

"Does that work for you?"

"Yeah," he said. "I'll tell them to expect you about 12:30 again?"

"Check. You'll come get her around five?"

"Check check. What are you guys up to today?"

"Just the usual. See you tomorrow at five."

"Uh… um, see you tomorrow." Daniel sounded surprised by my terse answer.

I felt a stab of guilt. Not about cutting the call short but about the fact that it was surprising. Annoying as it was, it was a good thing my mom had pointed out that I was getting too comfortable with Daniel, otherwise I might not have realized it was my fault Brooke had wedding fantasies. I needed to break those bad habits before she started designing invitations.

We made a trip to get Brooke after lunch the next day as planned. Instead of the usual pigtails, she had one braid in the back. It was not a typical braid. It was a crazy fancy French braid. She told me her dad had made it with four sections of hair instead of three. Piper wanted the same thing, and I didn't know how. I thought about calling Daniel. He couldn't be the first person I turned to, not even when it made sense. I searched online for instructions. After a while, the girls got bored watching me try to find appropriately simple instructions. Piper told me I could learn and do hers that way another day. They went off to Piper's room while I spent time with Emmet.

I was lining up dominoes for him to knock over. Piper was into dominoes, and we'd been having issues with him knocking them down before she was ready. I hoped I could train him to be a little more patient, though I'd settle for removing enough novelty that they became less interesting.

Then I got something interesting, a call from Tim. I hadn't thought about him since Maddie mentioned him on Friday. This time he did ask me out. Maybe a different guy was exactly what I needed to put a little distance between me and Daniel. Maybe if I had someone else to think about, I wouldn't be spending so much time thinking about how I wasn't supposed to be thinking about Daniel. I agreed to meet Tim for dinner Wednesday night.

Then I went back to thinking about Daniel. Only for practical reasons. It was nearing five o'clock. I told Brooke her dad would be coming soon so the girls needed to clean up their art supplies. I could control how long I lingered at pickup, but I couldn't exactly kick Daniel out. I could only be sure Brooke was ready when he got there.

"Hey, Daniel," I said as I let him in. "The girls are in the kitchen." I led him straight through.

Brooke held up a picture of a girl wearing a dress and cape with pigtails down to her knees. "Look, Dad."

"Is that you?" he asked.

"Of course." She held up a second picture nearly identical to the first except the girl had yellow braids instead of brown. "This one's Piper."

"Very nice," Daniel said. "Grab them both so we can take them home."

"Aw. Can't I stay and make one more? I want to draw the troll we're fighting."

I held my breath. If Daniel agreed, we'd end up sitting together waiting for the girls. Maybe I could get Emmet to want to read books. I couldn't talk and read at the same time.

"Sorry, honey. You know I have that thing tonight, and we need time to make dinner."

I was about as relieved as Brooke was disappointed. I exhaled too soon though.

"I just heard from Grandma," Daniel said to Brooke, "and she's feeling worse and isn't going to be able to watch you. I'll have to call Brad and Kim to see if I can drop you at their house instead."

"All right." Brooke collected her papers and did a farewell bow to Piper with them clutched against her chest. Then she stopped only two steps from the table. "Hey, wait," she said. "Can Molly babysit?"

"Molly's been watching you all afternoon," Daniel said. "She's probably sick of you."

"Dad." Brooke said with one word that he'd just attempted his lamest joke. Ever.

Daniel smiled but refrained from laughing out loud.

"Can you, Molly?" Brooke turned to me. "Please."

I wanted to say no. I wanted to say, "Piper, you need a new friend because extracting myself from proximity to Daniel is proving even more challenging than I expected." But my instinct was to help when someone needed my help. My conscience told me there was nothing else I needed to do that evening. And Daniel was going out anyway. I wouldn't be signing up to spend time with him. I'd be signing up to spend time with Brooke, which might help her understand that me not marrying her dad wasn't because I didn't like her. "I don't have plans," I said, mostly to Brooke. "I can watch her if you want me to."

"That's generous." Daniel appeared to consider the offer while Brooke gave her most plaintive smile. "And it would be so much more convenient for me."

I could see he was only hesitating to give me a chance to back out. I might as well make it easy on him. "What time should I be there?"

"It's from seven to nine, and I only need five minutes to get to the church. And you can put her to bed halfway through so it shouldn't be too hard."

"Yea!" Brooke waved to Piper and to me. "See you soon." She grabbed her dad's arm and tried to drag him to the door, apparently afraid something or someone might change his mind.

Stephen was expected in about an hour. That would give me enough time to run home to check on my mom and arrive at the Devoras' in time. And not a moment too soon. Hopefully, I could time it to arrive just as Daniel was leaving.

****

My mom was feeling better. She'd been up and around most of the day. She still only wanted to have plain crackers for dinner. I heated up some leftovers and told her I was going to babysit for Daniel.

"Interesting," she said. Brooke wasn't the only one who could pack a lot of thoughts into one word.

Against my better judgment, I asked about those thoughts. "What do you mean?"

~ 67 ~

"It's just interesting that you say you're trying to spend less time with Daniel and yet you've volunteered to spend an evening at his house."

"Mom. I'm *babysitting* for him. I'm going to his house, but he's going to be somewhere else."

She gave one of those motherly nods that said she wasn't agreeing with what I said; she was simply acknowledging that I said something.

"I already admitted you were right about how things were looking between us. But now… I thought maybe spending a little time with Brooke would prevent her from thinking that me backing off has anything to do with her."

"Doesn't it?"

"No," I said.

"You said one of the reasons the relationship would be too complicated was because he has a child."

I stabbed my fork into my food and shoved the rice and chicken around without really looking for a bite. I did not appreciate having my words deliberately misinterpreted. "There's a difference," I said, "in avoiding a complicated *situation* and avoiding a person associated with it. It's not about Brooke personally."

"That's a subtlety that would be lost on a lot of people."

"It isn't lost on me."

Mom looked at what I was doing to my dinner and seemed to decide to drop the subject. "I'll probably turn in early tonight so I might be in bed when you get back."

"All right, Mom. I'll see you in the morning then." I cleared away the food I hadn't finished and took the light bag to babysit.

Brooke answered the door when I got there. "Come in, come in," she said, waving me into the house and straight to the kitchen. The game of *Life* was half assembled on the table.

"Are you getting this out or putting it away?" I asked.

Her expression turned timid. "Will you play?"

"Sure."

She grinned and grabbed a white plastic house to attach to the board.

I threw my bag in a corner and took a seat at the table.

"This will be so much better than playing with Dad," Brooke said.

"Why is that?"

She sighed and stopped what she was doing to give me a serious look. "He criticizes it the whole time. He says it makes no sense to suddenly add a second peg after you get married because shouldn't you know someone *before* you get married. He complains about some of the prices not being realistic. And he *always* says it's a bad idea to teach kids that you win at life by having the most money." She rolled her eyes and picked up the plastic bridge. "I have to remind him over and over that it's just a game."

I smiled to myself at how easily I could picture the scene she described. "Where is your dad anyway?" I hadn't seen or heard Daniel since I entered the house.

Brooke just shrugged at me and asked what color car I wanted.

"Uh... red, I guess."

She nodded and began to count out some money.

I heard footsteps on the stairs and turned to say hello to Daniel as he approached us.

"Molly's here," Brooke said.

"Yeah, I see that." Daniel smiled at me before he addressed Brooke. "I hope you checked to make sure it was someone you knew before you opened the door."

"Of course I did." Brooke bit her lip as though she was stopping to consider if she really had checked. After she answered his question.

I think Daniel noticed that but chose not to nag more at the moment. "So I'll be back just after nine. You won't have any trouble entertaining yourself after she's in bed?"

"I'll be fine," I said.

He nodded. "Make yourself at home. Good night, ladies."

As soon as her dad was out of the house, Brooke added a blue peg to her car. "You'll have to wait until after your car finishes college to add a guy," she said, "because you didn't meet anyone to marry while you were in college."

"Aren't you the one who just said this is only a game?"

She flashed a smile with cute little dimples. "But it's still fun to pretend it's real."

"All right." I looked over the board as I hadn't played since I was a kid. "I'll add a boyfriend peg when I get over the mountain."

Brooke nodded and let me spin first, which seemed like consolation for agreeing to play with her. That made me want her to know I was enjoying the game. I didn't have to pretend. I simply tried to be more demonstrative than I otherwise might have been. And we talked while we played. "I'm glad you suggested I babysit tonight," I said, "but you might be old enough to stay by yourself before long."

"Dad let me twice already. Just when he had to go somewhere quick." She lit up at the thought, then began to dim. "I didn't like it. It's... a little scary to be home by myself."

"Yeah?" I was pretty sure I looked sympathetic without trying because I completely understood. "Do you think your gut was trying to tell you that you're not ready to stay home by yourself or just that you need to get used to it?"

She shrugged slowly. "Does it make me a baby if I'm not ready?"

"Only if I'm a baby, too," I said with a laugh.

Brooke asked what I meant with a severely puzzled expression.

"I live with my mom partly because neither of us wanted to live alone. We're both okay with being alone some of the time, but not all the time. And I think my mom is pretty old for anyone to call a baby."

"Is she as old as your dad?"

I shook my head. "Not quite. You've met my mom."

"I have?"

"Many times actually. She comes to get me at church after the donuts. Remember?"

Brooke continued to throw a blank face into the conversation.

"Your dad calls her Linda," I said.

"Oh!" Brooke began to nod. "I didn't know that was your mom."

I spun the wheel to distract Brooke from how hard I was trying not to laugh at her, and trying not to ask why she thought I'd called that woman Mom. Daniel had said more than once that children had an uncanny ability to pay attention to adults when it concerned them and not when it didn't. I'd love to share this example with him.

"Won't she have to live by herself when you get married?"

We'd gotten in a few more turns since talking about my mom, but I still knew who Brooke meant. That wasn't why I took my time in answering. I wanted to be sure we were speaking in general terms. "Well... I don't currently have plans to get married," I said, "and if I ever do, it usually takes at least several months to plan a wedding. That would give my mom time to get used to the idea of living alone or find a roommate or... something."

She nodded thoughtfully while I waited to find out what was going through her head. What if she asked me directly about her dad? I needed more time to come up with a good response. Would she understand and accept it if I simply said he was my friend and not my boyfriend?

The moment of silence stretched on until Brooke said, "It's your turn, Molly."

"Oh." I relaxed and refocused on the game. I couldn't help but be a tiny bit flattered when Brooke named her imaginary daughter after me. It was eight o'clock by the time I won. She took it well and also agreed easily to let me put it away while she got ready for bed.

I didn't expect any trouble putting her to bed. I went upstairs after I cleaned up the game to ask Brooke if she needed anything. I found her sitting on her bed – in tie-dyed pajamas – holding a book. She smiled expectantly at me.

"Have you done everything you're supposed to do to get ready for bed? Teeth clean?"

She gave me a dutiful nod. "Now you read. Daddy reads one chapter a night."

"Ramona?" I said as I took the book from her. "This's a good one. But won't your dad be upset to miss a chapter? Maybe we should read something else?"

"No. I'll tell him what happens. That's what we do when Grandma reads."

I sat next to her and opened to the bookmark. She climbed under the covers after the one chapter, and I turned out the light as I left the room. Being summer, it wasn't completely dark yet.

I'd only been upstairs twice before. One time the girls wanted to show me a fort they'd made in Brooke's room before I took Piper home. The other time was a tour, though not of the house. They were playing zoo and insisted on taking me and Daniel around to the exhibits they'd set up.

Brooke's room was at the end of the hall near the bathroom. I passed the other two rooms on my way to the stairs. One was a small spare bedroom currently used as an office and storage area. Brooke's old crib was propped against one wall in pieces. There had been a stuffed monkey under the desk the other time I'd stepped into the room. I looked under it and was not surprised to find nothing. The surface of the desk was clear except for a neat stack of folders. I was glad nothing was out because I already felt nosy and didn't need more temptation.

Temptation, unfortunately, was lurking right outside anyway. I stepped back to the hallway meaning to only glance at the last room. Though it hadn't been included in my tour, I knew it was Daniel's room. The door was open. The windows inside were dripping light on the floor of the hallway like a welcome mat.

I was standing on that patch of light before I could talk myself in or out of anything. I would look in but I would not go in, I rationalized. He had dark brown sheets and a tan blanket. The bed was unmade, but the room didn't look messy. There was nothing on the floor and the bedside table held only a book and a pair of light blue hair elastics. A television peeked out at me through a partially open door of an armoire in the far corner. I backed away and stepped softly down the stairs.

I went into the kitchen for a drink. I got sidetracked by a framed piece of paper on the wall. I'd read it several times before. I read it again because it always made me chuckle. It was something Daniel saved from Brooke's preschool days. The teacher had asked the three-year-olds questions about their dads and filled in their answers.

On the first line that asked for the dad's name, Brooke's answer was "Dadiel," like Daniel with a cold. I knew why Daniel liked it. He just thought it was funny. It always made me think that I liked his full name. I dated a guy in college who went by just Dan. By dated, I mean I went on three dates with him. I didn't see anything really wrong with him. I just felt as though I should be more excited so I said we shouldn't go out again. It was early enough in the relationship that it could hardly be called a relationship. I didn't imagine he'd be that attached. I was wrong. That happened at the end of my first year of college, and it took me two years to agree to a date with anyone else. I should have waited longer, but I wasn't going to think about what happened with Aaron.

I kept reading Brooke's old paper to bring my spirits up. She said that her dad was ten feet tall and weighed about twenty pounds. According to the very young girl, his favorite food was tacos, his favorite book was all of them and for fun he liked to "throw me on the ground."

Daniel told me she meant play wrestling. He was glad that the teacher had understood that and no one felt the need to call Children's Services. He'd still been a little embarrassed to have it hanging on the wall at the preschool. At home, apparently, was a different story.

I was still smiling when I opened the refrigerator. I helped myself to a bottle of root beer. I took it and the book I was still holding to a good place on the couch. I didn't start at the beginning of the book. I picked up where I'd left off after reading to Brooke.

# 9

Daniel had pretty good timing. He came in when I had only two pages left. I smiled at him and held up the book. "I'm almost done," I said.

He nodded and went into the kitchen. I heard the refrigerator open behind me as I moved to the last page. Daniel sat in a chair opposite me. I closed the book and set it aside. He leaned forward so that his elbows rested on his knees. He held a bottle like mine between his hands.

I needed to leave. I was only supposed to spend time with Brooke. Now that Daniel was back I felt... well, what I felt was an intense attraction to the man I was trying to distance myself from. I definitely needed to leave.

"So how'd it go?" Daniel asked.

I guess I at least owed him a babysitting report fist. "Fine," I said. "Or great, really. It was time for bed by the time we finished the game and she didn't give me any trouble about that. Then I went snooping around your house."

"Mm-hmm." Daniel bit back a smile. It looked as though he assumed I was kidding but wouldn't care if I wasn't.

"Mostly just the fridge," I clarified as I reached over to grab my drink. The bottle was not even half empty. I thought I should finish it before I left so it didn't go to waste.

"I'm glad you made yourself comfortable," he said. His eyes scanned my seat on the couch... and the empty place next to me.

I exhaled slowly, then took another sip to finish that drink faster. I hoped the best way to keep things friendly and focused on the fact that I was there for Brooke was to talk about her. I told Daniel he needed to send me a link to where he learned the latest braid. I filled him in on the details of our board game, how she'd added a blue peg early like he'd taught her and that I liked the sound effects she made as her car arrived at certain spaces.

"I hope you really didn't mind playing," Daniel said. "It was my fault she already had it out when you got here."

"Did you tell her that was the best way to guilt me into playing?" I was teasing, but I wouldn't entirely put it past him.

He looked, for a moment, as though he was going to take credit. Then he shook his head. "She was excited about playing with you, and I mentioned that you'd need to start right away to have time to finish before bed."

I nodded. "And how was your evening?"

"Does that mean, 'Was Josh there?'"

"It means I'm curious about your evening." I sounded more defensive than I intended. Daniel was attending a discussion series on the seven deadly sins. The guy who had talked him into going, Josh, had skipped the last two meetings. Daniel had been so funny about being "stood up" that I wanted to know if it'd happened again. But it wasn't the only thing I wanted to know. He didn't have to look so confident that he knew what I was thinking.

"Come on, Molly, you can admit it. You're not curious about my evening," he made little mocking finger quotes, "you're curious about whether or not Josh showed up, about whether or not he left me like chum to the sharks *again*."

I couldn't hide it. His chum reference told me the meeting had been entertaining, at least for me to hear about. "Okay," I laughed. "Was he there?"

"No," Daniel said. "It'd be fine if he just admitted he's a coward. But I know he's going to call me tomorrow, make some excuse, then ask what he missed as though he has any intention of showing up next week." He sighed heavily. "Today was envy."

I smiled and waited for the details. Josh was only a few years older than Daniel. Apparently, everyone else out-aged them by about two generations. Daniel told me after the first meeting that the older guys thought the younger ones were the only ones who still needed to learn a thing or two about the topics. It had felt like the two of them needed to defend themselves against all the ills of everyone under a certain age. I knew he exaggerated, but it couldn't be entirely in Daniel's perception if Josh kept skipping out.

"Well, I got a lecture on phones," Daniel said. He leaned back as though preparing to give a lecture of his own. "It seems that the most significant manifestation of envy in our culture, and specifically in my generation, is that we all need to own the latest model of cell phone. I'm not going to argue against phones driving a lot of keeping up with the Joneses mentality, but I do not enjoy being made to feel as though I am solely at fault. This one guy showed me a picture. He pulled out his phone and showed me a picture of a massive landfill of discarded phones. He didn't show it to anyone else. I was the only one who needed to see the results of my wasteful ways. And I'm not kidding when I say he was showing me this picture on a phone that is newer than mine."

"Oh, no. Did you point that out?"

"Absolutely not. If I had said a word, everyone in that room would have accused me of *envy*ing that phone. And I think they made some secret pact that now I always have to go first."

"Go first at what?" I asked.

"We have a list of discussion questions and for each one, ten pairs of eyes turn to me like, 'First let's hear what the young person has to say. Then the rest of us can sit around and discuss all the things he still has to learn. In other words, why he's wrong.'"

I thought he might be inflating the scene to get me to laugh. I enjoyed the description anyway.

Daniel watched me laugh for a few moments. "Three more weeks of this," he said. "But I'm only going to two. I already know that something very, very important is going to come up to make me miss the week on lust. Josh could not pay me enough to..." He waved his hand as though cutting the subject off like a weed with a lot of thorns. "Is your mom feeling better?"

I stopped laughing. I really didn't want to discuss lust with Daniel either. "She's definitely on the mend. Sounds like she's going back to work tomorrow."

"Good to hear," he said.

"What about your mom? Is she very sick?"

"She told me when I came to get Brooke last night that she was afraid she was coming down with something. She sounded worse today but wanted to babysit anyway. She's kind of stubborn and I had to insist she rest. I'm glad me and Brooke aren't showing any signs of catching it. Sometimes the flu takes people out like dominoes." His eyes softened. "Do you still feel okay? I should have asked that before I let you help."

"I'm fine," I assured him. "Speaking of dominoes though, I was standing some for Emmet today."

"Still think you're going to cure him?" Daniel tipped his head and raised an eyebrow to show how unlikely he thought that. "Dominoes are way too cool to knock over. Especially if someone else is going through the trouble to stand them up."

"Maybe. He seems to enjoy it even when I knock them down by mistake."

"I bet he likes the look on your face."

"What look?"

"I bet you get a very cute, 'Oh, shoot, look what I did,' sort of expression." He looked at me as though *he* would enjoy that.

I took a sip of root beer. Hopefully, something cool would keep the heat out of my cheeks.

"Kids like it when grownups make mistakes," Daniel said. He pointed to a picture of Brooke on the wall. "When I switched out Brooke's latest school picture, I somehow missed the nail when I went to hang it back up and dropped it on the floor. I could tell Brooke was trying not to laugh. Then I managed to do it again. She gave up and was doubled over laughing so hard. It was great. It's so hard to get her to laugh on purpose."

There were two pictures on the wall he indicated. One was that school picture. The other was a family portrait with Daniel, his late wife Kathleen and Brooke as a baby. Daniel had lost some weight. Probably not more than ten pounds or so, but it was enough that the rounded face in the picture seemed to exaggerate his youthfulness.

He followed my eyes but guessed incorrectly as to which of the people had my attention. "She's changed a lot, hasn't she?" he said.

"She has." I nodded. "But I was looking at you. I can't believe how young you look there."

Daniel frowned. "As opposed to how *old* I look now."

"No." I tried not to laugh. Surely he wasn't old enough to be sensitive about his age. I still remembered being surprised when I met him. Maddie and Stephen were both over forty. I think I assumed without even realizing it that Piper's friends' parents would all be roughly the same age. "I meant that you look even younger in the picture than you actually were. Young to be holding a baby."

He kept looking at the picture as he said, "Kathleen and I got married right out of college. I thought we should wait a few years before we started a family, save up and try to prepare more. Kathleen wanted kids right away. She said she wanted to be young enough to play with her grandkids. I wasn't really convinced we were ready until I actually held Brooke the first time. All of a sudden, I thought I'd been crazy for wanting to wait for that moment."

Daniel turned to me with a smile, but his eyes had already gone serious. "When Kathleen died, all I could think was how she'd planned to be here for her grandkids and wasn't even going to be here for her daughter. It probably sounds weird, but it was that thought that kept me going. I just knew that if Brooke's mom wasn't going to be here, then her dad needed to be here a hundred percent.

"I read the parenting books that I'd been letting Kathleen tell me the gist of. I found a job that had flexible hours. I even started eating better. Of course my mom was an even bigger help in the beginning than she is now. I don't need to be the only one Brooke can rely on."

"What about…" I wanted to ask about Kathleen's family. Daniel had mentioned once that they weren't local, but I didn't know anything else.

Daniel nodded at me to say he was open to a question.

"I'm curious about Kathleen's parents. You haven't talked about them and I wondered… how involved they are."

"Yeah, that's... kind of hard. Kathleen and I met while she was away at school. We dated only a year and I'd met her parents twice before the wedding. Then... well, we just – because of the physical distance mostly – didn't have enough time to develop much of a relationship before Kathleen died. They've never disliked me, as far as I know, or tried to blame me or anything like that. But with the distance and without Kathleen as a bridge..." He shrugged. "I send them pictures of Brooke a couple of times a year with quick updates on what she's doing, and they always seem grateful to get them. They don't reach out much otherwise. They did visit once, with some serious awkwardness. That's just where we are."

"Those are difficult circumstances." I did understand, though it wasn't nearly the same. I wished being family made me automatically closer to my brother and sister. We all got along. We just didn't put much effort into the relationships because we were leading different lives. "Did you find the parenting books helpful?" I asked. "I've read a few this past year now that the topic is sort of job-related for me."

"A little." It was a self-deprecating smile, and it only showed up for a moment. But I did like those dimples. "I'm sure I learned some," he said, "but I usually felt like I was nodding along with anything that reinforced what I already thought or disregarding anything that didn't."

I laughed because the thought was familiar. "Well, judging by the fact that Brooke is a good kid, you either had good ideas or got very lucky."

"I'm willing to accept a little of each." He shook his head. "I don't know where she gets the serious streak though. Sometimes I really don't know if she's on the verge of getting upset or just trying to mess with me."

"I think she just has a different sense of humor."

"You mean she thinks being serious is funny?"

"Maybe." I shrugged weakly. "I might not know what I'm talking about though."

"Well..." Daniel sat back and sighed. "I do know she's serious about wanting siblings and that's breaking my heart because it's one thing I can't do for her. At least... not by myself." His eyes flickered to the floor and tentatively over me.

It was awfully brazen of Daniel to mention babies to me and make me think about… things that led to babies. And he dared to look all nervous and… inviting about it. How did we even get on that subject? Brooke thought I might be the answer and that was why I'd resolved to put space between me and Daniel. Two days ago. Two measly days. I'd made the resolution two days ago and had already failed. *Oh, God, forgive me for this.* My drink was long gone. I'd been sitting there talking with Daniel for over an hour. I'd failed so horribly. "I… I didn't realize how late it's getting." I jumped up as I said it. "I should get going."

I took the empty bottle to the kitchen, rinsed it, and set it in the recycling bin. The bin was under the sink. It was completely out of sight, and I knew where it was. I was too comfortable in the house where I didn't belong.

Daniel was waiting for me by the front door, hands in his pockets, looking uncertain about a lot of things. "I, uh… I don't know the going rate for babysitting."

"I've already been paid in root beer."

"I didn't think you'd let me give you anything, but… it's better to…"

I nodded. It *was* better to be clear about everything. Honest about expectations. "I don't expect to be paid for helping a friend."

"For helping a friend." Daniel repeated my words. He hesitated on the last one as though his mouth was exploring it. His eyes suddenly began to plead with me and the expression held me captive. I knew I should leave. I had a pretty good idea what he was about to say, and I knew I shouldn't let him. I didn't want to leave though. *God, help me.* I didn't ever want to leave.

Daniel put his hand up and brushed his fingertips across my cheek. He whispered, "It would be so simple, Molly." Then he waited for me to respond.

I stood there waiting myself, for what I couldn't say. All the arguments about why this beautiful intimacy was a bad idea were right there in my head. I could not get a single one of them to come out my mouth. I only waited.

Daniel seemed to take my silence as a positive response because he started talking a little louder and a lot faster. "I know I have a kid. But she already likes you. And she respects you. She wouldn't make things complicated for you. We *like* simple here. We like our schedules. We have pancakes every Sunday and elephant puke every Friday. My goodness. I never thought I'd be trying to convince a woman that I'm boring enough but... I am completely boring. There are no surprises here. Very little would change practically speaking, except... maybe..." His gaze dropped to my mouth, then came back up with a question.

My brain was too clogged with emotion to go anywhere logical. All I could summon was curiosity. What would it be like to kiss Daniel? How many more seconds did I have to wait to find out?

He came about halfway towards me before he stopped again, still searching my face, still wanting me to tell him it was all right.

I shook my head slightly, trying to indicate that I didn't know what to say or what to do.

Or at least I thought I shook my head. Maybe I didn't because Daniel did kiss me. The moment his lips made contact with mine, I shut my brain off. I didn't want to think about anything. I refused to think about anything besides the fact that I had never been more certain that my heart was beating. It declared its presence with thumps so forceful I was desperate to know if Daniel felt the same intensity.

We were kissing deeply while my hands roamed his chest, ostensibly to find the pulse I'd felt as soon as I touched him. Then my brain tried to resume thought, tried to register the thought that it wasn't only a physical response. I might be in love with Daniel. That was not. Allowed. To. Happen.

I wrestled with my head for two more seconds before I jumped away and opened my eyes. "No."

Daniel was backed up against a wall. Though I was talking to myself, he looked startled and possibly as though he was about to apologize for *my* mistake.

"I'm sorry," I said first. "I shouldn't've done that. I shouldn't... I shouldn't even be here. Good night, Daniel. See you at soccer on Thursday."

I yanked open the front door and raced down the steps, kicking myself for what seemed like the stupidest thing I could have said. See you at soccer practice? That's what I would have said if I hadn't just kissed him. It's what I would have said if I hadn't just muddied the water and made things as complicated as I'd been trying so hard to avoid. But after the kiss, somehow, it became the wrong thing to say.

Tears had dropped on the front of my shirt by the time I got home. I sat in the garage with my hands on the steering wheel and my head in my hands. I tried to pray away the guilt. *God, I thought I needed forgiveness before and now... I screwed up so badly. I'm so sorry. What do I do? How do I...? What happens now?*

No answers came. I remembered that feeling I'd had a few days ago that something was coming for me. Now it felt like a big, fat told you so. I'd been playing with fire, and there was a part of me that knew it all along.

# 10

I was sitting by myself listening to a love song. I guess it counted as a love song because there was passion in the words, though they weren't directed towards a person. The deep male voice sang about the salty air and raging water of the ocean with a longing that must be attributed to love. The exaggerated emotion was kind of ridiculous. I wanted to laugh at it. I wanted to laugh at something because I was so tense. But I was too tense to laugh.

I was thinking that I kissed Daniel yesterday. He'd kissed me first, but I had definitely kissed him, too. I'd been reliving the scene in my head all day with confusion and panic and mostly denial. I wanted so badly to pretend it hadn't really happened. Now things were going to be messy and awkward between us. And I had to wait a whole day more to find out exactly how messy and awkward.

In the meantime, I had a date with someone else. Maybe. I was sitting in a restaurant called The Sleepy Crab where we had agreed to meet at 7 PM. Ten minutes after seven I was still alone. I pulled out my phone to contact Tim and was seized by a sudden fear that I was the one who was wrong.

When he suggested Wednesday, I assumed he meant the next day. But that was short notice. What if he meant the next Wednesday? How embarrassing would it be to call or text a guy I barely knew to let him know I was a week early for a date? I'd sound desperate. I'd sound a lot more eager than I actually was.

I didn't know Tim well enough to be excited about seeing him. I was only excited about the idea of seeing someone, the idea of dating someone, someone who could drive away thoughts of kissing Daniel.

"Still waiting, huh?" The guy who had brought me a drink when I sat down was back at my table.

"Yeah," I said. "I'm going to give him a few more minutes."

The server snorted as he walked away, clearly thinking I was pathetic for not admitting I'd been stood up. I wasn't going to let a teenager with blue hair make me feel bad. If I was wrong about the day, it was Tim's fault for not clarifying. I texted him: You meant this Wednesday, right? Where are you?

I unrolled and rerolled my silverware in the napkin while I waited.

Tim responded with: I'm still coming.

That was a terrible answer. One, because it was a terrible answer. Two, because it set me to thinking that Daniel would have given a much better answer. He'd have apologized *before* he was late, and he would have let me know about when to expect him. Comparisons were not helping anyone's situation. Although at least I now had justification for being annoyed with Tim. I could channel my tension in his direction and not at myself for complicating another relationship with a kiss.

I really wasn't going to be able to stop thinking about that, was I?

Tim managed to arrive before 7:30. Barely. He sat down and said, "Glad you waited."

"Hi," I said. I sort of wanted to ask what kept him, but he didn't appear in a rush at all. I had a bad feeling he had no reason I wanted to hear.

Mr. Blue Hair returned and asked Tim what he wanted to drink.

"Coke," he said.

"I suppose you're ready to order?" The server looked at me impatiently.

I looked at Tim. "Do you know what you want?"

"Oh. I guess I should open this." He picked up the menu with a carefree chuckle.

I glanced up to say we'd need a minute. The young server didn't give me a chance. He was already in the middle of an extreme eye roll and mumbled, "Bet you're glad you waited," as he went away.

He'd seemed to judge me as a loser when he thought Tim wasn't coming and now implied I could do better. Apparently, Mr. Blue Hair was not on anyone's side.

I put my elbow on the table and propped my chin on my hand as I faced my date. With his eyes cast down at the menu I took a moment to look him over, trying to form an opinion of his appearance. He seemed to have a lot of spots on his face. Not freckles, just darker spots, and I wondered if there were more under the beard. It was longer at his chin and almost pointy like a villain beard. The hairs were also slightly deeper brown than what was on his head and that seemed backwards to me, even though I couldn't think of that many guys who had lighter facial hair. I thought I shouldn't try to form opinions while cranky.

I quit analyzing random details and considered Tim's overall appearance. I could objectively say that he was a decent-looking guy, but I didn't feel any particular pull of attraction. It was possible that was because I didn't know him well enough. Time to work on that.

"What looks good to you?" I asked.

Tim turned to the back of the menu without looking up. "I always get the bacon burger."

"Always?"

"Yeah." His eyes came up to meet mine. "It's good. Have you tried it?"

I shook my head slowly. He seemed to miss the point of my question, thinking I was suggesting he branch out rather than wondering why he was reading the menu if he already knew what he liked.

"So how are you?" he asked.

Hungry. I'd already pushed back my typical dinnertime before he pushed it back another half hour. I was trying not to be negative though. "Not bad," I said. "The kids and I took some chalk outside today and it got pretty hot. We survived though."

"I would think chasing after a couple of rugrats would be an exhausting job. Do you like it?"

"Most of the time. I suppose the level of exhaustion depends on the kids. Your niece and nephew are, I think, relatively calm."

"You decided?" The server was back at our table with a notepad ready. He appeared to jot down our requests but didn't say another word. I couldn't be sure he wasn't writing snarky comments while he planned to bring us whatever was easiest. I wasn't doing a wonderful job keeping the negativity at bay. In fact, I was beginning to wish I'd stayed home to listen to Strauss with my mom.

Tim started talking about his job. He worked for a marketing company. The impression he gave was that he did nothing all day but answer emails from very impatient people. Then his phone pinged a text, and he gave me a play-by-play of the conversation.

"It's Benji," he said. "He's a friend from work. He wants to know when I'm going to be there. I'm going to have to ask him where 'there' is." Tim put the phone down for a moment but not long enough for either of us to say anything.

"His house?" He squinted at the phone as he picked it up and started typing. "Right. I'm supposed to pick up some extra bricks he has. Maddie said she'd like to put some around the flowers at the front of their house. It'll probably be after nine before I can get over there. I suppose that will be too late to take them to Maddie tonight."

Tim set the phone on the table again. He said, "Do you have siblings?"

"I have a brother and a sister," I said.

"Older or younger?"

"They're both older."

"So you're the baby, too?" He sighed. "Do they still treat you like you're a baby even though you're, you know, thirty?"

"Well, I'm not thirty *yet*." I knew he had just turned thirty because I saw the old man birthday card Maddie bought to tease him when it happened. I hoped he wasn't really sensitive about it. I didn't know what else to say because I didn't feel like my siblings treated me differently than they treated each other. Though that may have only been because we didn't spend much time together. Foreign countries and remote lifestyles were not exactly relationship glue.

"But you still know what I mean?" Tim tapped his phone to make it light up. "I'm sure Maddie is about to act like I'm not capable of bringing over a few dozen bricks."

Did he just text Maddie, too? I still wasn't sure what to say. While it sounded like a nice thing he was trying to do – helping one person get rid of something he didn't want by giving it to another person who did want it – I had to question the appropriateness of making those arrangements while on a date. Especially when it already didn't feel like a date. Or at least not a first date.

"Benji says nine is too late can I come over tomorrow and…" Tim looked at me as though I wouldn't believe what he was about to say. "Maddie says, 'What bricks?'" He typed away while I sucked the last bit of my drink from my glass. When I set it back in the puddle, the glass hydroplaned nearly two inches. I tried to make it happen again because the sliding glass was more entertaining than what was going on across the table from me.

"Maddie suggests I bring them by on Saturday." Tim shook his head as he typed as though he didn't understand the suggestion.

A pretty woman with a blond ponytail showed up with two fresh drinks. "Griffin got a little tied up and asked me to deliver these," she said. "Your food should be ready any minute. Can I get you anything else in the meantime?"

"No, thanks," I said, offering her an appreciative smile. She had an open friendliness about her that was nice to see even if only for a moment.

Tim eventually finished his other conversation and turned to me. Unfortunately, Maddie had told him about the brush with lice and that's what he asked me about. It made me remember how what started as a near crisis ended as a fun day with Daniel. I smiled as I thought about him saying he'd dip his hands in lice water for me, until I realized that he might have been seriously flirting with me. I'd ignored a lot of warning signs before Brooke hinted of her hopes for me and her dad. I should have backed off sooner. I could have prevented that kiss I couldn't stop thinking about.

I chose to let my growling stomach distract me. "Doesn't it seem like our food is taking a long time?" I asked.

"Is it?" He checked the time but didn't look convinced by the fact that it was nearly 8:30. I suppose he'd have to know what time we ordered for that to mean anything. "If you point out our server, I can flag him down and ask for you."

I looked around but didn't see him.

"Is it that guy?" Tim indicated a man who looked around forty.

"The guy waiting on us is much younger," I said. "And I doubt he dyed his hair."

Tim wrinkled his eyes as though he had no idea what I was talking about.

"You didn't notice that our server's hair is light blue?"

"Really?" He clearly hadn't noticed.

When we finally saw him enter a side door, Tim waved him over to ask about the food. The server just shrugged at us and said he was working on it. The friendly blond woman brought it out a few minutes later. It was good. Tim ate so fast I wasn't sure he had time to notice the flavor. Not that I minded. The server did manage to bring the check promptly. I don't think Tim noticed how grateful I was to call it a night.

# 11

I was a little nervous walking into the Youngs' house. I hadn't completely thought through what it might mean to go out with Maddie's brother. I worried now that it might be uncomfortable if she asked about the evening. She brought it up in just the right way.

The kids were eating breakfast as usual. Emmet was still in his pajamas.

"The little guy slept in this morning." Maddie nodded at him over her coffee. "Thought I'd go ahead and feed him and let you get him dressed after breakfast."

"No problem," I said. "Morning, Piper."

She smiled at me. "What kind of braids is Brooke wearing to practice?"

"Uh... I don't know." Daniel had texted me about a TV show after I got home from the evening with Tim, something about a camera angle obviously not showing a game people were "playing." I'd agonized over a simple rating response. I wanted to backpedal to friendship and wasn't sure that was possible. Was any contact encouraging? Or was ignoring him rude no matter what? I tried to relax after the exchange stayed short. Didn't work. "Why don't you pick today," I said to Piper, "and I'll just let her dad know?"

"Okay. I like the fishtail ones."

"Good choice." I hadn't learned that new thing yet. I'd text Daniel later. There would be no need for back and forth if I simply sent him a little FYI.

"So Molly..." Maddie set down her mug and gave me a direct stare. "Please tell me that my brother was not texting me while he was out with you."

I scraped my teeth over my lower lip. "Do you want me to lie?"

She smiled and groaned at the same time. "Sometimes I wonder what to do with him. I mean, I love Tim, but I don't understand where he got the scatterbrain gene. The rest of us are all like type A people and he's…" Her mouth moved silently before she found words to fill it. "We were talking at the barbeque and I mentioned that I thought a brick border would look nice around the flowers and several weeks later he texts me out of the blue asking when he can drop off some bricks. He didn't say anything in between about knowing someone with spare bricks or asking how serious I was or…" She sighed heavily. "He's just the kind of guy where everyone always says, 'His heart is in the right place, *but…*' There's always a but. I mean, I'm pretty sure he'd give me a kidney if I needed one, but I'd have to tell him the surgery was scheduled an hour earlier than it really was to have any hope he'd show up on time."

Maddie smiled at her own assessment, threw back a last swallow of coffee and jumped up from the table. "And now I need to get moving if I want to be on time. Stephen is out of town again. Kind of a last minute trip so I don't remember if I told you. But I'll try not to be too late tonight, and he'll be back tomorrow."

I nodded as she left the room. It didn't hurt to confirm the schedule, but she had told me about the trip. Or at least when he'd be out of town. I didn't know anything about Stephen's job except that it was some sort of government thing. At some point, I realized how I didn't know anything and joked that he was keeping all the details classified. He said I watched too much TV. But he never did tell me anything about his job. I chose to assume it was uninteresting rather than dangerous. I claimed the seat Maddie had vacated and looked at Emmet.

"I see you, Molly," he said.

"I see you, too." That sort of became our theme for the day as we kept coming back to Hide and Seek. It usually frustrated Piper when Emmet wanted to hide with her. Either he was getting better at finding his own places or she was getting better at helping him.

We arrived at the soccer field with Piper in her fishtail braids. Daniel had responded to that information with a very simple "okay." For that I was glad. There was nothing awkward or uncomfortable about okay. I could imagine that everything was about to be A-okay, okey-dokey and hunky-dory. We were just going to pretend that kiss hadn't happened. I would say hello, maybe exchange a few comments about the weather, and then I'd mingle with the other parents like I should have been doing from the start.

Piper ran ahead of us. Emmet was walking next to me so I could approach slowly because he had short legs and not because the butterflies in my stomach were flipping out at the sight of Daniel. Piper and Brooke greeted each other with their customary bow then dashed onto the field.

I stopped with Daniel a little more than arm's length away and pointed out a rock I thought Emmet would find interesting. He immediately squatted to examine it. I looked up and said, "Hi."

"Hi," Daniel said, shifting his weight against the effort of one word.

I hated that the butterflies were right about the level of tension between us. "I think it's less humid this week." I wished I had a hygrometer to stick in front of Daniel. I'd force him to look at the numbers and take those soul-piercing eyes off of me.

He nodded briefly at my observation then glanced at the field.

I happily followed his lead. The girls seemed to be having an intense conversation, probably another adventure.

Daniel inhaled rather loudly next to me. I sensed that he was about to say something, something not casual.

"I think the Braid Defenders are at it again," I said first. "Who do you think they're saving this time?"

"Uh… could be anyone." Daniel dismissed my topic. I still sensed that he was trying to bring up something I didn't want to talk about. It didn't happen. We didn't have to talk about something that didn't happen.

"How's that rock coming, Emmet?" I bent to focus my attention on the little guy. Sort of. I remained very much aware of Daniel, how close he was, how he looked towards the sky for help when I turned away from him. But now I looked like I was paying attention to Emmet. The rock I'd pointed out to him was partially buried, and he was trying to dig it out with his weak little fingers. "Maybe this stick will help get it out." I handed him what was actually a piece of bark.

Emmet poked at the ground while I said things like, "Try on this side" or "You almost have it" or anything I could think of to look like I was helping and delay standing up again.

Eventually he had the rock in hand and was turning it over to appreciate all sides. I could only marvel at a rock for so long before it would be obvious I was avoiding talking to Daniel. I cast my eyes back to Piper as I stood. My brain clicked off my own situation entirely. "Uh, oh," I said.

Daniel looked that way, too. "What is it?"

"I think the girls have had a fight." They normally lined up next to each other for drills. Brooke had her back to Piper with several teammates between them and Piper had her arms crossed in an angry posture.

"I think you're right," Daniel said. "They both look upset about something."

"I guess… or I think we should wait and see if they can work it out themselves. Unless you think one of us needs to get involved?"

"Not yet." He tipped his head to the side while he thought it over. "They'll probably have forgotten whatever it is by the end of practice."

"I hope you're right."

"What about us?"

Nuts. He caught me with my guard down. I tried to build it back up but couldn't assemble a coherent thought.

"Can we work this out, Molly?"

"I, uh, don't really think we have anything to work out."

"Are you mad at me?" Daniel asked. "If I misread something and need to apologize, just tell me so I can do it." There was something almost desperate in his voice. It crumbled the wall I was trying to rebuild. Honesty and communication. Those were the tools that kept relationships healthy. I summoned the courage to use both.

"I'm not mad." I faced Daniel so he'd see the sincerity. "And you didn't misread anything. I just..." How many times did I need to say that I wanted to avoid complications? "I just think it's better if we pretend that what happened didn't happen."

"I don't think I can—"

"Molly! Molly!" Piper had taken hold of my hand and was tugging on it. "I'm going to be goalie. Come watch me. Come on!"

She was pulling me towards the net at the other end of the field. The way she looked back made me think she was deliberately pulling me away from Daniel. Since I felt rescued, I didn't bother to question her motives. I called for Emmet to come with us and tried to offer Daniel a friendly wave.

He waved back. Unfortunately, I could read his expression all too well. It said he was letting me run away but only for the moment. That conversation was not over. I had the weirdest impulse to laugh at his persistence when it should have annoyed me.

Piper positioned me next to two other women watching the practice and then ran to take her place in front of the net for the scrimmage.

The closer woman was wearing a T-shirt so baggy it hid her shorts. I hoped she was wearing shorts. She said, "Hello."

"Hi," I said, trying to include the other woman as well.

Her beautiful tight spirals bounced when she offered a friendly nod in return.

"Which kids are yours?" I asked. I'd paid enough attention the last few weeks that I thought I already knew which kids went with which adults, but I couldn't think of anything more creative to start a conversation.

"I'm Ryan's mom." The curly-haired woman gestured towards the field. "He's the one in the blue socks."

"Lucy's mine." The closer woman pointed to a girl running past us. "I'm Sarah."

"Molly Hartigan," I said. "I'm with Piper." I just sort of glanced at the goal since they'd seen her bring me over.

"She's your... daughter?" Sarah looked doubtful.

"No, she's... I'm her nanny."

"Oh!" Something like relief washed over Sarah's face. "So you might actually be as young as you look, and I don't have to hate you."

I didn't know what to say to that. She seemed to be trying to be funny so I forced a smile. The other woman had taken a step away from us and appeared absorbed in something on her phone. "This is Emmet," I said. He was using the rock he'd dug up to pound a patch of grass.

"Is *he* yours?" Sarah asked. Something in her tone made me wary.

"He's Piper's brother."

She nodded, looking from Piper to Emmet and back, before she said, "There must be seven or eight years between them. I suppose he was a little oops?"

The gap between Piper and Emmet might have been larger than the average between siblings, but I'd never asked Maddie or Stephen if it was intentional. Given that she was nearly forty-two when Emmet was born, I thought it just as likely or more so that they'd had trouble. I still never asked. "God doesn't make mistakes," I said. "He makes babies."

Sarah gave a short laugh that sounded as forced as my earlier smile had been. We both turned to the kids' practice and managed to drift away from each other. I ended up sitting in the grass next to Emmet watching for bugs when I wasn't watching Piper. We had five more weeks of soccer practice. Would they all be this stimulating now that I couldn't pass the time talking with Daniel?

Piper still seemed to be ignoring Brooke when they left the field. I waved goodbye to Brooke and to Daniel. They returned the gesture and Daniel called, "Keep defending the braids."

Rather than her typical battle against a smile, Piper turned and shot him a dirty look. Daniel's eyes widened in surprise. The little dents in the sides of his face gave away that he was the one trying not to smile. I understood. It wasn't a dismissal of her feelings. She typically had a shy streak around Daniel though so open hostility was unexpectedly amusing. Brooke simply rushed ahead of him to their car.

I got Emmet buckled without saying anything. Then I began the drive back wondering what to say. "You and Brooke seemed to be having some trouble today." I paused after the observation and heard no response from the backseat.

"Do you want to tell me what happened?"

"No." Her word was adamant. What I saw in the rearview was sadness though and not anger.

It seemed best to give her some time. We were sitting together at her kitchen table when she was the one to bring it up again the following day. Emmet was down for a nap. I was looking over some recipes Maddie had planned, and using them to make a shopping list. Piper was coloring a picture.

Quite suddenly, she went from filling in some trim on a dress to making violent green lines over the page. She put down the colored pencil so forcefully it rolled off the table almost as if she'd thrown it.

"Piper?" I hoped she could tell I was concerned and not scolding.

Her eyes were red and she was clearly trying not to cry. "I want to be friends with Brooke again, but I can't."

"Why can't you?"

"Because..." I could see she was struggling for words. "I just can't," she finally said.

"But you still don't want to tell me what happened?"

A shaking head was my only reply.

"Okay. It's hard to help if I don't know what the problem is though." I thought for a moment, and also waited to see if Piper might decide to share. My best guess, since she said she wanted to be friends again, was that she was afraid Brooke wouldn't accept an apology or she didn't know how to ask. "If you think there's something you need to say to Brooke that's difficult, it might be easier to write it down."

"What do you mean?"

"Some things that are hard to say, like maybe I'm sorry, you can put in a note to the other person and still make things better."

She nodded but also grunted at me. It seemed she understood and either didn't believe me or didn't think it would help in her case. Then she asked if she could help me make the shopping list instead so we dropped the subject. Later, when I was playing with Emmet, I considered asking Daniel for advice.

I had my own problem though, that I was trying to reestablish the boundaries of our relationship. But this had to do with the girls and that felt like something within the appropriate bounds. As long as I was careful. I texted: Has Brooke told you what the fight was about?

Daniel: No. Said she couldn't tell me because it involved me? Do you have intel?

Me: No luck here either. Piper seems to want to make up though.

Daniel: Same here. I say we leave it alone a few days.

Me: You think it will resolve naturally next time they see each other?

Daniel: That's my hope.

It felt like a reasonable hope. And I trusted Daniel's judgment. I hoped that the soccer game on Saturday would provide the opportunity, but it was rained out. I didn't see any of them all day.

# 12

"Wow. This is a treat." That Sunday started thoroughly different from the last one. I got up to find my mom in the kitchen making pancakes.

She smiled at my enthusiasm and said, "Grab a plate."

I helped myself to a few steaming pancakes. I thought of Marie as I doused them with small circles of syrup and spread it with the back of my fork. When we were little, my sister used to challenge me to eat pancakes without letting any of the syrup drip onto the plate. I don't know how or why she came up with that. I couldn't shake the habit even years later.

"Is that enough for you?" Mom asked.

I considered the deliciousness versus the calories and possible donut later. "Maybe just one more."

Mom nodded. "I still can't get the recipe down to only two people. Remember how many I had to make when your brother was a teenager?"

"It was like he was in an eating competition. With himself."

"Last time I talked to Matthew, he mentioned he'd lost a few pounds. I guess he's eating a little more sensibly these days."

"Well, as far as leftovers go, I'll have no problem warming some up for breakfast tomorrow. Or as many days as it takes."

"They're better fresh," Mom said.

"Maybe." I enjoyed a bite. Mom's pancakes had the perfect fluffy texture. "But in this case not quite as good is still really really good."

She smiled at the flattery. "You look very nice today, by the way." Apparently, she wanted to share. "I think that pink dress is my favorite of yours."

"Thank you." It was my favorite, too. It had white flowers along the bottom and a full skirt that flared out if I spun fast enough. I felt like a carefree kid when I twirled it, but I mostly refrained from that indulgence. At least when anyone else was watching.

Mom put down the spatula. "That's all of them. Do you mind cleaning up when you're done? I still need to get ready."

"I'll take care of it."

"Thanks." She put the pan in the sink and flicked a messy braid over her shoulder. Mom was still wearing a nightgown and slippers. It always amazed me how quickly she could go from looking like she fell out of bed to completely refined for the day. "I'm excited this morning after being sick last week," she said. "I don't remember the last time I missed a Sunday mass."

Mom stopped halfway out of the kitchen and sent me an apologetic glance. The last time must have come back to her as soon as she stopped talking. She patted my shoulder as she resumed her exit.

We both knew when she last missed church because it was my fault. And Aaron's fault. Mostly Aaron's fault. Or maybe mine.

Aaron was the last guy I dated. We met near the end of my third year of school. We talked only a few times with mutual friends before we both went home for the summer. He called me only two days after I returned for the last year. He said he'd been thinking about me all summer and asked if we could get together.

I tried to take it slow, avoid labels. I did like him though and we gradually spent more time together. When he asked to make our dating official, it seemed too late to stop the drift. We looked like a couple to everyone, including him. He introduced me to some new foods and new experiences. He was fun. For a while.

After a few months, his relentless pursuit of something new began to exhaust me. He picked me up one day for what I thought was going to be a simple lunch. We ended up driving around for two hours looking for a restaurant he'd heard about but didn't know the name of. We never found it. He still thought it was a worthy adventure. I thought it was a waste of time and gas and that wasn't just the hunger talking.

Aaron constantly talked of wanting to see as much of the world as possible. He said that being surrounded by people and not knowing what any of them were saying would be fascinating. He never seemed to notice that my reaction did not say fascinating. But I dismissed warning signs that we weren't good together, too. I'd already hurt a few guys and worried I was being overly picky.

I had to admit once and for all that a future with Aaron was not right for me when I got lost on a disc golf course in February. We had dropped everything to try it out when someone told Aaron there was a course not far from the campus. Not far was actually over an hour of driving. He'd never played and needed that experience. Apparently.

We made it through nine holes, and I became more cold and more miserable and my aim worse at each one. Aaron wanted to call his brother at the end to talk about how cool it was that no one else was crazy enough to be out in the snow. Yes, it was snowing. I told him I'd meet him at the car and began back at a jog. I hoped the exercise would warm me up. Somehow I ended up back at the ninth hole where I'd started running. I made a few more wrong turns before I made it back to the car. I knew Aaron would be waiting for me, and I knew I was not running towards him. I knew our relationship was over, or it should be.

I convinced myself that our incompatibility was obvious, so obvious that Aaron must see it, too. I didn't have to break up with him. I only had to wait for him to end it. But a month later we were still together. I grew desperate for him to see the faults between us and tried to show him. I became argumentative. I made sure my favorite movie was playing every time he came to see me. I showed up late when we made plans. Finally, I woke up on a Sunday morning with a splitting headache. I called Aaron to tell him that he'd have to go to church without me. A reckless impulse made me say it was because I was hungover. I knew he wouldn't approve. His father was a recovering alcoholic.

I didn't approve of the lie though. I called him back immediately. I confessed it was a regular headache and didn't know what made me say otherwise.

I'm not sure if it was the lie or the retraction that sent Aaron over the edge. Regardless of the exact cause, he definitely freaked out. He called my mom. He called *my mom*. He told her he was worried about me because I'd been acting erratically. He was convinced I was either suffering a mental breakdown or dealing with a trauma I hadn't told anyone about. Maybe even both.

Mom hadn't heard from me in a few weeks, which was unusual, because I was too embarrassed to talk to her about the trouble between me and Aaron. She had no cause to think Aaron was prone to unreasonably freaking out. Mom got in her car and drove the four hours to school.

Her sudden arrival left me no choice other than to admit I'd been trying to get Aaron to dump me. Mom was sympathetic. She mostly listened. But I knew my approach was childish even when I didn't get a lecture. At the end of her visit, she reminded me that Aaron knew she was coming to see me and that he was probably expecting to hear from one of us.

I promised I'd handle it. I called Aaron almost as soon as Mom left and asked if I could come over to talk. The version I told him was that I was acting weird because I knew our relationship wasn't working out, and I didn't know how to say that. He said he could have forgiven me for breaking his heart but not for humiliating him in the process. I'd caused a ton of extra hurt by trying to avoid it. When he accused me of doing it on purpose, of enjoying the spectacle of stringing out the end, I didn't attempt a defense. When he called me names meant to injure, cruel titles I deserved, I took them as rightful punishment. It didn't matter to either of us that I never intended for us to be a couple in the first place.

Neither had I intended for my mom to give up her entire Sunday to my love life. I was determined that the current Sunday would have nothing to do with my love life. I wanted to think that was because I did not have a love life. But Daniel would be there. I could remember so clearly how it felt when he kissed me, and he seemed to think we needed to talk about that rather than continue trying to forget.

My plan was to avoid him as casually as possible. I let my mom go ahead of me to the parish hall while I stopped in the restroom after church. That gave the coffee line plenty of time to grow. The parish hall was swarming with activity by the time I entered it. I stood in the doorway and watched a teenage boy slowly deliver a dangerously full cup of coffee to the nearest table. I had my doubts, but he managed to set it down without spilling any.

My mom was with her usual group. I moved past them to my own usual table. Daniel had been trying to catch my eye since I walked in. I smiled and nodded at him as though I'd just noticed. Then I slipped my eyes to his right and back with approval. Brooke was next to him and Piper was next to her. The two girls were engrossed in conversation as though the argument, whatever it had been about, had never occurred. Daniel backhanded his forehead with exaggerated relief.

"Good morning, everyone," I said.

I got a lot of nods and greetings from the rest of the bunch. They filled in the table so that the only empty seat was between Daniel and Maddie and because they'd added a chair for me, it was close to both of them. There was already a cup of coffee for me in front of that chair. I sighed. Daniel was trying to foil my plan to spend half the morning in the coffee line. Of course he didn't know that. I still sort of wanted to glare at him for being so considerate. I went to a backup plan instead.

I dropped my bag into the chair to claim it without actually sitting down. "I'm just going to say hello to Monsignor Loy."

I took the white paper cup towards our pastor. He was standing by the donuts, well-positioned to speak to as many parishioners as possible. Monsignor Loy was an older man, very thin with a Santa-like white beard. He laughed at something as I approached. The sudden animation caused my feet to freeze where I was.

This man was very near my father's age. Two or three years older as a matter of fact. Yet he looked so sharp. So alive. I didn't know what the other person said to make him laugh, but Monsignor Loy did. His eyes said he understood what was funny, why it was funny, and even the importance of finding that humor in life. The last time I heard my dad laugh, it had been strained and unnatural. He laughed because he thought someone expected him to laugh.

I'm not sure how long I stood anchored by the thoughts in my head or at what point the priest moved to be standing in front of me.

He smiled when I noticed him. "You look like a lost sheep today," he observed. His tone was gentle, inviting a conversation with no expectation of one.

"I, uh… I'm not lost," I said. "I was on my way to say good morning to you actually."

"And got distracted by the donuts?"

I looked at the treats nearby. I was about to shake my head except that now that he pointed them out I was distracted. They'd been fairly picked over. In the closest corner of the box, however, was a perfectly round cake donut with a perfect drizzle of chocolate frosting. I had decided not to have a donut after I ate that extra pancake. Why did that one have to look so deliciously perfect?

"I apologize for tempting you," Monsignor Loy said. "Was there something you wanted to talk to me about? Other than the quality of the morning, I mean."

"No, I just…" I just wanted to use you to avoid talking to someone else. That would sound terrible, even if it was mostly true.

"It is possible to be lost even when you think you know where you are."

Well, I was definitely not thinking about donuts anymore. I was too confused. Was I supposed to respond to a general metaphor or was he hinting at something more specific? My mom talked a lot so the latter was a possibility.

Monsignor Loy brushed aside my cluelessness. "You are visiting your dad later?"

"Yes. Right after coffee."

"I'll pray it goes well."

"Thank you," I said. "Have a nice day."

He nodded and turned to the next person waiting for a chat. I took a sip of the coffee then walked slowly back to the table, drowning in uncertainty. On the one hand, Daniel wasn't going to say, "Hey, what did that kiss mean to you?" in front of his daughter and everyone else. On the other hand, it happened because I failed at creating distance. Making another excuse not to sit next to him felt dishonest. Sitting there pretending I wasn't tense and preoccupied also felt dishonest. It seemed to me that I had a devil and an angel whispering to me to sit and to not sit, except that I couldn't tell which advice was coming from which source.

I put my hand on the back of the folding chair intending to pull it out and remove my bag when Stephen jumped up and suggested to Emmet that they head outside for a bit. Emmet grinned at me as he climbed from his chair and that was enough for me to follow. Daniel watched me leave. I was sure of that without looking back.

There was a preschool behind the church and a small fenced playground next to it. Stephen scooped Emmet onto his shoulders as soon as we were outside, which caused the toddler to squeal in delight. He set him down at the gate to the playground and watched him run towards the equipment. "Needed some fresh air?" I asked.

"Needed to plant a new idea," he said. "Emmet kept asking for another donut. A playground makes an excellent distraction."

"Yeah." I smiled as Emmet grabbed a railing and began to climb steps that came almost to his short little knees. If I found steps that high, would I think it was fun or too much work? "Do you know, uh… since the soccer game was rained out yesterday, are they going to extend the season for a week or anything?"

"I hear they plan to have everyone play two games next Saturday, but…" Stephen shrugged and worked his face to show doubt. "I don't know how that's going to work."

"That's an interesting plan."

He shrugged again.

We watched Emmet in silence for a moment.

"*Old Yeller* was on the classic movie channel last night," he said. "Have you ever seen that?"

"No."

"The thing I don't get is how the boy at the end thinks Old Yeller is his dog."

"What do you mean?" The only thing I thought I knew about the movie was that it was about a boy and his dog. Was I wrong?

"Well, you know they have to shoot him, right?"

"No." Though I did now. "Why?"

"The dog gets sick so they have to, you know, put him out of his misery. It's frontier time so that means shooting him. Anyway, the kid says he'll do it because he was his dog, but it was the younger brother who found the dog."

"He had a younger brother?"

"Yeah. And the little one is also the one who trades the real owner a toad for the dog. So how does the older brother think it's his dog?"

"I don't... That sounds like a good question." So the movie was about two boys and a dog? And a toad? I thought Monsignor Loy was trying to confuse me.

Emmet had moved to the swings and was calling for someone to push him. Stephen moved forward to take up the task. I watched for a minute before I went back inside. My mom would probably be ready to leave soon. She was, in fact, asking Daniel where I was as I returned to the table.

He pointed to my bag on the chair. "I think that means she wants us to believe she's coming back."

"I'm right here," I said, trying to ignore the way his phrasing hinted at something devious.

"Are you ready to go, honey?" Mom asked.

"Sure." I picked up my bag and waved to Maddie, Piper, Brooke and even Daniel, a testament to the fact that I was not ignoring him.

Daniel picked up his cup and drained it as he stood to walk towards the exit, and a trash can, with me and my mom. Now who was making pretenses?

"Molly, are you busy tonight? Brooke wants a rematch at *Life*."

Using his own daughter to get me over there? I wasn't going to fall for it. "Not today," I said. "I just... have stuff to do.

Tell her to bring the game next time she visits Piper. All three of us can play."

Daniel nodded, tossed his cup, and let me go out the door without another word.

I was afraid my mom might have quite a few words for me though. Her eyebrows were lifted in question even while she began to squint against the sun. Was there anything I could say to get her to *not* say anything? There probably wasn't.

"Did something happen?" she asked.

I wrestled with an answer for a moment. I wasn't going to lie and say nothing happened. I also didn't want to tell her that not only did I let Daniel kiss me, I'd responded more than a little enthusiastically. My mom was not getting details. "Daniel knows now," I said. "I think he was getting the wrong idea and now he knows that I think we've been spending too much time together and that I'm trying to sort of dial things back between us."

"Hmm." Mom studied me like a detective examining a crime scene.

I squirmed and hoped I was only squirming on the inside.

"As much as I like to hear that you listened to something I said, you may have missed the point. I wasn't trying to suggest you dial things back."

"I know, Mom." I thought I might be too old to roll my eyes at my mother, but apparently I was not. "How many times do I have to explain why we can't, um… dial things forward?"

Mom laughed. I had the feeling she wasn't laughing at me trying to make dial things forward a saying as much as she was laughing at something *she* wasn't going to explain again.

I accepted the impasse and got in the car for the ride to Creekside. Mom, also, did not bring up Daniel again before we arrived at our spot under the shady tree. I was thinking about Monsignor Loy again in the silence of the elevator ride, about how he said I looked lost, about how my routines were my map to life, about how visiting the shell of my dad every week still didn't feel routine. And I was thinking about Daniel even when I wasn't talking about him. I was thinking about how I never wanted to give up the routines that involved him and about how angry I was that the situation had gotten off course.

~ 105 ~

I blew out a calming breath as the elevator binged then opened. I concentrated on the pattern of the carpet as usual until we arrived at Dad's room.

Mom knocked. We waited.

The only answer would come from a staff member and the door would have been open if someone else was in the room. We waited anyway.

Then Mom opened the door and called, "Hello!"

I followed as she began to point out the day of the week and how that meant she wasn't alone.

"Hi, Dad." I walked forward and put my hand in his. I didn't feel that reassuring squeeze. "How are you today?"

Mom started talking about Marie and how she was letting herself get excited about the baby. She'd put her last call on speaker and I'd tried to join in the conversation. I didn't want to talk about my sister's baby with my dad though. I still thought it might be a cruel topic when he wouldn't be here when the little one was born. Mom went on describing a quilt she was making for the baby though. She seemed to think Dad would want to hear about it. I didn't know who was right. Dad couldn't tell us.

We wheeled him down the hall for lunch later. Mom couldn't get him to hold the fork. But his drink was a high calorie shake. He'd take a sip if she put the straw in his mouth. We were sitting and talking with another resident, someone Mom knew fairly well from her more frequent visits. As we were finishing, the woman asked if she could tell Mom something about her kids. I picked up on the implication that she wanted to tell Mom something about her kids *alone*.

"I'll take Dad back and meet you by the elevator in a few minutes," I said.

Mom nodded agreement. Her older companion smiled appreciatively at me.

The wheelchair was easy to push. I tried to think that and not that Dad was a lot lighter than he used to be. I entered his room and positioned him in front of the TV. Mom usually left it on for him when he was alone. "Do you want to watch something on TV, Dad?"

I picked up the remote. "No news. I know you think you like it, but we don't want to ruin your Sunday. Let's see..." I flipped through a few channels until I found the History Channel. I could never remember the number there. "Here we go," I said. "I know you're still a documentary fan. I hope this isn't one you've seen before. So I'll... I'll see you next week. Bye, Dad."

I put my hand in his. When his fingers remained still, I used my other hand to wrap them around mine. His eyes lifted slightly to my face. I could see my silhouette reflected in the pale blue and I knew he saw me looking at him with love. Even if he didn't understand or even know me, I knew he saw. An unexpected peace settled over me as I felt that my visit mattered.

# 13

Shortly after 8 PM that Sunday, I noticed that it was after 8 PM and couldn't seem to stop looking at the clock. Brooke would be in bed. If I hadn't been so quick to reject Daniel's invitation, I could be over there settling everything. Yes, I began to avoid him as soon as I realized he wanted to talk about what happened rather than forget it, but not indefinitely. I only wanted to avoid him long enough to organize my thoughts.

I'd already explained, more than once, that I didn't want a complicated relationship. I didn't know what else to say. At first. Now I'd had time to think about it. I knew I needed to ask for his help. We were getting too comfortable together and the kiss proved it. I couldn't quietly pull back. I needed to be upfront about reestablishing boundaries and Daniel could help with that. He could help me keep our focus on Piper and Brooke's relationship. Together we could keep this simple. Or at least make it simple again.

My phone was sitting on the counter between my bags. It and a few other necessities I kept in the small bag that I stuffed inside the larger diaper bag when I was on nanny duty. I rarely carried nanny things for Piper. Maybe I could look forward to a less complicated system when Emmet got a bit older. I stared at the phone, thinking about calling Daniel. We could get the talk over with. He'd probably be grateful to me for the initiative.

My eyes scanned between the bags in my hesitation. Something white caught my eye sticking out of the smaller one. It looked like paper. Had I forgotten to throw away a receipt, or was it something else I'd forgotten I was carrying? Either way, I needed to investigate. I needed to find the answer. I needed a reason to put off that phone call.

I opened the bag wide and found an envelope labeled "To: Molly." What was that? I would have noticed a letter when I pulled the bag out for church so it must have been inserted since, probably during that time I left the bag next to Daniel in the parish hall. I pulled the letter out and unfolded it.

Dear Molly,
Brooke thinks we are going to get married. I thought I should make sure that's not what you think. I will never marry you. Don't ever talk to me about this.
Sincerely,
Mr. Devora

I recognized the handwriting from all the times I'd watched Piper do her homework. I took the letter to the next room and handed it to my mom. "Look what I just found," I said.

Mom's eyes crinkled with a mix of amusement and alarm. "Could this have been written by Brooke or was it definitely Piper?"

"I know that handwriting," I said. "It was Piper. Should I confront her about this or tell her mom or what?"

"Intentions count for something, especially with kids."

"Thanks for the cryptic response, Mom."

She smiled at my sarcasm. "Do you think Piper would write that just to be mean or do you think she might have had a plan?"

It was a rhetorical question. "So you think I should go easy and just ask her about it?"

"Remember that book you read a few months ago that said asking kids to admit when they've done something wrong – especially when you already know they did it – puts them on the defensive, tempts them to deny it?"

"Yeah?"

"Don't ask her if she wrote the letter. Tell her you found it and ask if she wants to talk about it. Or you can ignore the advice of someone who's raised three kids."

Mom's advice made sense to me, and so did a few other things. Brooke thought I might marry her dad. Piper evidently didn't want that to happen. It seemed likely that's what they'd been fighting about. Piper probably believed she could stay

~ 109 ~

friends with Brooke if she put something between me and Daniel.

I waited until Emmet was napping the next day to ask so Piper and I could talk without interruptions. She asked if I would play a game with her. I brought the game and the letter to the table. She had seemed fidgety all morning, guilty perhaps, and I hoped she might even feel better after we talked.

I set the paper with her words in front of her. Her head dropped and her lips trembled.

"Piper," I said, "I'm not mad at you, but I know you wrote this and I think we should talk about it. Putting words in someone else's mouth is dishonest. I know you know that so I'm concerned that something is really bothering you to make you do this."

She nodded slightly but stayed quiet.

I tried to be patient and also offer some encouragement. "Does this have something to do with what you and Brooke were upset about?"

Piper kept looking at the table. Eventually, she said, "Brooke wants you to marry her dad."

"Why does that bother you?"

"Then you'd be her stepmom."

I needed a little more help. I might have suspected Piper of having a crush on Daniel if she hadn't given him that dirty look at the park. This just didn't sound like that kind of jealousy, if it was any kind. "I'm sorry. I still don't understand why that would be a problem."

"If... if you were Brooke's stepmom, then you'd have to take care of her and then... you couldn't take care of me and Emmet anymore." Her voice faded with each word.

"Oh!" I shook my head. "That's not... Your mom has a job other than taking care of you, right? So doesn't it make sense that I could have a job other than taking care of Brooke?"

Piper finally looked up and stopped talking to the table. Her eyes were squinted in doubt and very shiny from tears. "It's not the same thing."

"Yes, it is."

"No, it's not. Brooke goes to camp now, but she said if she had a stepmom she wouldn't have to anymore. Camp is the same time you're here."

Rather than get into logistics of something that wasn't going to happen, I decided to lay it out nice and simple, just the way I liked everything. "Let's make this simple," I said. "Just for the record this probably isn't going to happen anyway, but if Brooke's dad ever asks me to marry him… I'll tell him I'll only say yes if working out a way for me to still be your nanny is a condition. Does that make you feel better?"

Her smile answered for her.

"Great. Let's forget about this," I dropped her note into the recycling bin, "and get this game started before Emmet wakes up."

I really did forget about the note until shortly after Stephen came home from work. When he was traveling, I usually made dinner, fed the kids (and sometimes myself), then stuck leftovers in the fridge for Maddie to eat later. When Stephen was in town, I typically got the meal started and he got home in time to finish and serve. Finishing dinner that night meant pulling it out of the oven. It still had twenty minutes to go. Stephen put Piper and Emmet to work setting the table.

"Are you staying?" he asked me.

"Not tonight." It seemed best if I didn't rush out the door the moment one of the parents came home. It gave me a chance to remember if I had anything specific to report about the day, and it let everyone sort of shift gears more gradually. I'd at least sit at the table if Stephen walked in really close to dinnertime. I had a few minutes to spare today.

"Are we still a well-oiled machine around here?"

"Pretty much," I said.

"No accidents?" Stephen's eyes dropped to Emmet then back to me.

I shook my head.

"All right, buddy. That's at least a full week. Give me five." He held his hand out to his son.

Emmet was on his way to the table with a plastic cup in each hand. He looked hesitantly between them for a moment before he tapped Stephen's hand with the bottom of one of the cups.

He giggled about it the rest of the way to the table. Then he started tapping the cups all over the place.

Stephen tried to distract him by asking where the cups were supposed to go.

Emmet just kept tapping and laughing.

Piper put her hands over her ears. "Make him stop!"

That felt like a fine time to make my exit. I found my bag and pulled my keys from the smaller bag inside before I returned to the kitchen to say good night. The kids paused in their noise to say goodbye. Stephen was standing near the recycling bin, peering into it. I realized that Piper's letter had landed face up and he was reading it. He looked puzzled for a moment, then he seemed to shake off any confusion or interest as he turned to wave at me. I kind of wanted to thank him for being the only person – other than perhaps Emmet – who didn't care about the status of my relationship with Daniel Devora. I thanked him by not mentioning it.

****

Mom got home after I did. She hadn't had a chance to visit with Dad during her lunch so she stopped at Creekside for a while after work. I warmed up a few of those pancakes for dinner because I'd been too sleepy to think of them in the morning.

We sat at the table talking longer than usual for no particular reason. It was after nine by the time Mom put on some music. I was just going to read for a few minutes and then get ready for bed. My phone buzzed at me before I found my place in the book. It was a text from Daniel. But it wasn't one of those fun comments on TV mistakes.

Can I come over?

He should be on his way to pick up Brooke from his mom's house. Why was he asking to come to mine instead? I texted: Now?

Daniel: Please. Let's talk about this.

I knew what this meant. I had gotten over my urge to call him to get the talking over with though. I thought we'd wait until Thursday and chat naturally at the soccer field. With witnesses. My heart rate was speeding up at the thought of facing him though. Perhaps it would be better to do it now, with little warning, little time to work myself into a full panic. I sent: Okay.

"What's up?" Mom asked.

I guess I didn't need a lot of time if Mom could already see I was agitated. "Um... Daniel's coming over."

"Now?"

"Yeah."

Mom pushed herself from a comfortable chair, switched off the music and took a few steps to face me. "Molly," she said, "do you want to tell me what's going on?"

The words were already on my tongue, just waiting for me to open my mouth. "He kissed me, okay? And I want to pretend it didn't happen. Daniel is not on board with that perfectly logical plan. He thinks we need to talk."

"Oh." Mom smiled knowingly. "I'll hide upstairs when he gets here to give you two some privacy."

"It's nice out. I'll just wait for him on the porch."

"You'd have more privacy, like from the neighbors, in the living room."

"I don't want to know where your head is, Mom," I said, trying not to sound like I was the mom, "because we don't need that kind of privacy for a *conversation*."

Mom's expression crumpled. "You're still determined to keep the relationship platonic?"

"Yeah, I would think my *mother* would want that."

She smiled at my attitude. "Chaste, yes. Platonic? Neither of us wants that for you. He's a keeper."

"It's like you don't even hear me when I talk. How many times do I have to explain that dating Daniel would be too complicated? It'd get messy with the girls if it didn't work out. And if it did, there's just too many... it would be a bad idea because... it just can't happen."

Mom put her hand on my arm, gently. "Do you think there's any chance you're trying to come up with excuses because you're a little bit scared?"

There it was, the nerve more exposed than any other. "Of course I'm scared, Mom," I burst out. "I hurt everyone! He's a widower with a child. That is not a heart I want to be responsible for. Not with my track record."

"Oh, Molly. Come here." Mom wrapped me in a hug. I let her only so I could hide my face while I wiped away the tears. Once I gave in though, it felt nice.

"You can't blame yourself for every failed relationship," she said. "You were careless with James, but not intentionally cruel. And you were seventeen. The others were not your fault. Not even Aaron. It wasn't anyone's fault when those relationships didn't work out. There's always a risk when you open your heart to someone. Daniel knows that. I think we can say he knows it better than most, and he still seems to think it's worth the risk. In fact, it seems to me that he thinks *you're* worth the risk. Is that a man you want to walk away from?"

"No." I pulled away and stiffened my spine. "But I have to. When it comes down to it, I'd rather break my heart than his."

Mom looked at me, biting her lip, clearly wanting to say something else and deciding whether or not to hold back.

The doorbell rang.

She said only, "Good luck," and turned to go up the stairs.

I inhaled sharply. How had Daniel gotten there so fast? Had he texted from the driveway or had my mom been trying to comfort me longer than I realized? I peeked out a side window to confirm the identity of the visitor. Daniel had his hands stuffed in the pockets of his jeans. I got the impression he was trying to make himself look as small and nonthreatening as possible.

I felt slightly light-headed. It occurred to me that I was still holding my breath. I let it out slowly and tried to steady myself against the door handle before I pulled it open.

"Hi," I said, then walked past Daniel to the porch swing without waiting for a response. I tipped my head to indicate he could have the seat next to me.

"Thanks for, uh… not avoiding me."

"You know I'm not avoiding you."

Daniel sat down and the swing rocked and creaked with the added weight. There were a few moments without words, only the sounds of the swing, during which I was sure he was trying not to laugh at me. "Care to tell me what else I know?" he asked.

"You know you're not as funny as you think you are."

He cocked his head and aimed the dimples at me. "How do I think one thing and know the opposite?"

"Exactly," I said. The panic had begun to dissipate during the banter. This was my good friend Daniel. I could tell him what I was thinking. "I'm not keeping my distance because of what happened last week." I said keeping my distance instead of avoiding you because that sounded more mature. And I said what happened instead of that amazing kiss because I was trying not to think that he was close enough that it could happen again. I was trying not to remember the warmth of his touch, the tenderness mixed with desire, the...

I snapped my thoughts back to the present. "I was already trying to sort of... pull away because I realized I was getting too comfortable and the... what happened before just proved I was right."

"Why is comfortable a bad thing?" Daniel asked. "I still don't understand why you're pulling back."

"Because it's... it's just for the best. This way no one gets hurt."

"If you don't want anyone to get hurt, you have to give me more than that. Don't leave me wondering what I did wrong."

"You didn't do anything wrong." The panic was rising again. Why was he trying to make me feel as though I was breaking up with him? That was precisely what I never wanted to do. My head was spinning and the conversation seemed to be going in circles as well. "I told you before that it was a bad idea. I told you that this," I waved my hand between us, "was a bad idea."

"You said we shouldn't date, but you haven't had any qualms about spending time together without anything official. I thought you wanted to avoid rushing into something. If you really meant that you know I can't make you happy, then I should know that. You can tell me the truth."

No, I couldn't. Tons of times when he had made me happy were flashing through my memory. I had to admit the real truth. I had to tell him the reason I couldn't let romance enter our relationship. I was horrible at romance. "The truth is… I've dated four guys in my life and it's always ended badly." I had to count James among the guys I dated because he thought we were dating and that was my fault.

Daniel tensed next to me. "I hope you're not about to tell me how they all hurt you because that's just going to make me angry."

"You'll have to get angry at me because I'm the one who made them cry."

"What does that mean?"

"It means exactly what I said. All four of them literally cried in front of me when the relationships ended. After the last one… I told myself it wouldn't happen again, that I would never hurt anyone like that again, that I simply would not get involved with *anyone* unless I could be sure it wouldn't end in heartache."

"How do you plan to make that guarantee?" There was a bite to his words. He clearly thought I was being unreasonable.

"I don't know yet. That's why I need to… I won't call or text unless it's related to Piper and Brooke and I'll start sitting with my mom after church on Sundays and…"

"You're going to avoid me so I don't get hurt?"

I nodded defensively against Daniel's disbelief.

"Don't you realize that's the only thing that won't accomplish your goal?"

"Don't say that!" I snapped. I was terrified by the implication and strong emotions propelled me off the bench swing. "Don't act like I'm doing something wrong. It isn't fair to make me feel like I'm ending a relationship we don't have. You can't—"

"Can't what?" Daniel stood as well and faced me, daring me to finish the thought.

I had intended to continue railing at him for accusing me of causing pain. A softness in his expression make me stop. It didn't look like an accusation, but it still suggested that I did have the power I didn't want. How had we gotten to this place I'd tried so hard to avoid?

"I can't love you?" he asked. His voice was quiet and hoarse. "Is that what you were going to say? That I'm not *allowed* to fall for you?"

I swallowed hard and began to shake my head. As absurd as he made it sound, he was not allowed to fall for me.

"I'm sorry I didn't wait for your permission." Angry sarcasm covered the apology and gave me a suffocating feeling as he walked off the porch.

A car door usually seems loud on a peaceful evening. Daniel's seemed to slam with more force than any I'd heard. I felt the noise in my chest with an ominous finality. But as he began to back down the driveway, he looked up and waved to me. As confused and emotionally wrung out as I was, I still recognized the hope in the gesture. I just didn't know what to do with it.

# 14

I didn't fully understand what happened. I started reading a book to Emmet and then I was closing the book. I didn't remember reading any of the pages in between. Emmet handed me the next book from his stack as though I hadn't missed anything. Apparently, a person's brain can only process the same words so many times before it starts doing it on autopilot.

The ability was not limited to toddler books. My mind was automatically calling up thoughts of Daniel. At least I was feeling better about the conversation of the previous night. I had convinced myself that Daniel was simply wrong. He didn't care about me the way he thought he did. When I said I needed to back off a little, that kissing him had been a mistake, I hurt his pride. Only his pride.

It wasn't my fault he mistook that for something deeper. I could almost relate to his mistake myself. I felt a weird sort of anxiety when I thought of seeing less of him in the future. It was only because we were friends, and I didn't like to adjust my routines. Throwing in some wounded pride might feel a lot like heartache. But it wasn't. Daniel was wrong.

I was sure he only needed some time to realize that. I wasn't sure what I needed. At the moment, I just wanted to get my head off Daniel and onto...

Oh. It was probably for the best that I wasn't paying attention to the book on my lap. Boring. And I meant boring for a book with one sentence per page.

I had taken the kids to the park first thing before it got too hot. After lunch, Emmet took a nap and Piper read to herself so quietly that I almost dozed off myself. Emmet appeared bright and refreshed as soon as he woke up, and I was still groggy from having closed my eyes for a few minutes. I felt like I was staring at a long afternoon.

"Can we make cookies?" Piper was suddenly standing in front of us aiming an ingratiating smile at me. I was still processing the question when Emmet climbed off the couch and raced to the kitchen. He was right though, I rarely said no to making cookies. And we hadn't made cookies for at least two weeks.

"All right," I said. "Let's make cookies."

Piper clapped her hands and dashed ahead of me. Maddie, with my help, kept the kitchen stocked with cookie ingredients. The church next door to Sacred Heart had a ministry that put together a dessert tray for a homeless shelter every week. When I made cookies with the kids, we each got one and the rest were donated.

"What kind do you want to make?" I asked Piper.

She already had a book of cookie recipes open on the counter. "This one," she said, tapping a finger on the page. "With sprinkles."

Of course. Piper always wanted to make something that needed to be rolled and frosted. No simple drop cookies.

"Sprinkles!" Emmet said. He was pushing a chair towards the cupboard where he knew the sprinkles were kept.

"Hang on there, Emmet." I redirected his chair to the sink and helped him wash up before we set up at the table. Piper was in charge of adding the ingredients, Emmet was in charge of stirring them together, and I was in charge of preventing disasters. Like the time Emmet stirred with the bowl too close to the edge of the table.

I rolled out the dough while the kids each chose a cookie cutter. Piper was going to make hearts, as always. Emmet was going to make trucks, or the shape he called a truck. I was pretty sure it was supposed to be a tractor. I was also pretty sure the cookies would taste the same no matter what we called them.

We had the first batch in the oven when my phone rang. My nerves tingled when I saw it was my mom. She wouldn't call me at work unless it was important. I grabbed a paper towel to protect the phone from my floury hands, then swiped across the screen with my cleanest knuckle. "Hi, Mom. What's up?"

"Molly, are you... with the kids?"

"Of course."

"I mean, are you at their house?"

"Yeah," I said. "Do you need something?"

"Well, I... no. I just called to tell you that... your dad passed away this morning."

"Oh." The news was not entirely unexpected, but it still left me speechless. The first response that came to mind was to ask what happened. But I already knew what happened. His body finally let go. His time had come. "When?" I asked, because I had to say something.

"Early this morning. I'm sorry I didn't call sooner. I... knew I'd see you tonight so I thought I should start with other calls and... then I felt bad for not telling you first."

"It's fine, Mom. Is there anything you need me to do?"

"Oh, no, honey. You know we did some preplanning. I already called the funeral home and the church. The funeral will likely be Friday... still ironing out details, but likely Friday." Mom sounded overwhelmed. That was difficult to hear because she was always so together.

"Do you need me to come home?" I asked. "I'm sure Maddie would understand."

"I'm not at home. I need to clean out his room at Creekside and it's taking me longer than I thought it would."

"I can help."

"No, I... I'd rather do it myself." Mom's voice got sharp for a moment before she took a breath. "I'm sorry. I do appreciate... just take care of yourself and I'll see you tonight."

"All right." I realized that the timer was going off as I put down the phone. Piper was staring at me as though she didn't hear the beeping either. Emmet was making beeping noises right along with it. I shut off the electronic beeping and Emmet quieted, too. The cookies were slightly darker than I would have liked but not burnt. Hopefully, there would be people who liked their cookies a bit more crisp.

"What's going on?" Piper asked.

"My dad died." As soon as the words left my mouth, I wished I'd taken the time to be less blunt. Emmet didn't fully know what that meant anyway, and Piper knew my dad had been sick for a long time. Still, they were children. I could have been softer.

"What does that mean?" Piper sounded timid. She knew what death was. What she wanted to know was what this particular death meant *to her*. How was it going to affect her life? While it was a selfish question, it was also perfectly natural. She was a kid. And it was, really, what we all wanted to know whenever anything happened. How would that event change our lives? The same question was in my head, and I wished someone could answer it for me as easily as I could for Piper.

"Well, I need one more minute to call your mom because I think I'm going to need Friday off for the funeral. Other than that, we're going to keep making cookies."

She nodded.

Emmet was making handprints in the flour. He was being surprisingly calm about it so I left him to it while I called Maddie.

"Molly?"

"Kids are fine," I started.

She laughed. "That's actually a great way for a nanny to begin a call, but what's going on?"

"I... well, I just got a call from my mom. My dad died this morning."

"Oh, Molly. Molly, I'm so sorry. Do you need to go home?"

"No. My mom isn't there," I said. "I'd really rather have the kids keep me company right now."

"Are you sure?"

"Yeah. But I think I'm going to need Friday off for the funeral and wanted to give you a heads-up about that."

"Of course. What time will it be?" she asked.

"I'm not sure yet. Mom just said it's likely to be scheduled for Friday."

"Got it. Let me know if you change your mind about leaving early today. I'll let Stephen know he might need to plan for that."

"Thanks. Bye."

Piper was still looking shy and solemn when I returned to the cookies. Emmet was lucky enough to be oblivious. The day mostly returned to normal as we got back into the groove of hearts and tractors. By the last pan, I convinced Piper they were tractors. Emmet still called them trucks.

****

Two days later, I hadn't cried over the passing of my father. It wasn't something I had told anyone but neither did I feel guilty about it. I had already cried the first time he talked to me as though I was a stranger. I cried when he didn't talk at all. My grief had gotten a head start.

I felt bad for my mom. She didn't put on her relaxing music those first two nights. She spent the time on the phone instead. It seemed to be her mission to personally notify everyone who ever knew my dad. She called friends, relatives, former colleagues and even a man who used to own the house next door. I heard names I hadn't heard in years as she went through her contacts.

She sounded reasonably upbeat as she chatted with each person, thanked them all for their sympathy and occasionally brushed away a tear that was undetectable in her voice. Only I saw the tears while I tried to read and not feel helpless. She still wanted to do everything on her own.

I planned to hide in my room if there was a third night of phone calls. But I had to get through soccer practice first. Daniel was the only person that I wanted to call and of course I hadn't. What kind of person would I be if I tried to lean on his friendship right after I rejected his attempt to make it something more? The situation did not change my stance where Daniel was concerned.

He had texted me that morning to say that Brooke was still enamored with the fishtail braids, and I let him know that Piper agreed. That was exactly where our relationship needed to be. I followed Piper as she ran up to Brooke. Her pigtails bounced on her back until she reached her friend. Then she pulled them forward for a Braid Defender bow.

They ran onto the field as I continued to approach Daniel. A smile jumped onto my face against my will. I think it was because I still hadn't gotten used to the shorter haircut. I could allow a friendly smile though. I planned to say hello and how are you. Then I would take Emmet to the other side of the field to watch.

"Hi," I said.

"Hi." Daniel smiled. It didn't look as though he had to wrestle with whether or not it was appropriate.

"How are you?"

"I'm fine." The smile disappeared. "But how are you? I saw your dad's obituary today."

"Oh. I'm okay. I'm… fine."

"Why didn't you tell me?" There was concern in the question, not blame.

"I, um…" He knew why so I just shrugged my shoulders at him.

"You could have told me. Is there anything I can do?"

"No. My mom's not letting me help much either so there's really nothing that… but, thanks."

Daniel nodded solemnly. He glanced towards the practice.

I took the break in conversation as my opportunity to move on. I led Emmet away from Daniel and away from other spectators. We found a lonely patch of grass. I dropped my bag to the ground and directed Emmet to some little cars in a side pocket. He took them out, and I watched him bang them together.

Then I noticed an extra shadow on the grass. I turned to see that Daniel had followed me. He looked amused by my surprise. "You didn't really think you were going to get rid of me that easily, did you?"

"What do you mean?" I asked.

"If I understood correctly everything you threw at me the other day… you do like me, you like to spend time with me, and you only want to keep your distance to protect me from you. Is that right?"

There was nothing in what he said that I could refute. I did not appreciate his condescending tone though so I merely stared back without saying anything.

"Well," he said, "I don't want your protection."

"What?" If he'd figured out that he was wrong about the extent of his feelings for me, he'd say he didn't need protection not that he didn't want it. Right?

The grin broadened and the dimples deepened, apparently in response to my confusion. I kind of wanted to tell him not to laugh at me, but he looked happy. That was enough of a reason not to start an argument.

"I've thought about it," he said, "and I'm not going to let you torture yourself for my sake. I can see that you don't really want to create this distance you're talking about. Not that anyone would blame you for finding it difficult. I am pretty great, right?"

Daniel paused to check for my reaction. I knew I couldn't resist a smile at the teasing so I tried to cover it with a quick peek at Emmet. He was still smashing cars into the ground. That was why I looked amused.

"But I get that you're worried about things getting messy if we change the rules," Daniel continued, "so let's not change anything."

He was willing to go on as friends? For a brief moment, my heart began to swell with gratitude. He was giving me everything I wanted and didn't think I could have. Then he mumbled two more words that crushed my growing excitement. "For now?" I said. "You want to stay friends so you can try to talk me into—"

"No." He stopped me with his hands out. "I promise not to try to push any boundaries or do anything to make you uncomfortable. I just feel I should be honest about the fact that I'm still hoping for more. If hope bothers you... then... tough tomatoes."

His struggle for the right words took the sting out of them. Or it would have if the words tough tomatoes carried any sting.

"I mean, if you try to ignore me, I'll just be hoping you change your mind about that so you'll need to live with hope no matter what." Daniel nodded as though convinced by his own argument. "You might as well live with it in the way that makes us both happier."

I nodded, but I also looked at the girls on the soccer field. "I don't know. I don't want to hurt Brooke either. She, um, she thinks we're going to get married."

Daniel smiled. That news wasn't news to him. "She also thinks she's going to be a professional artist and that she and her husband are going to have six kids, first three boys and then three girls all exactly one year apart. And her husband's last name will start with D because she wants to change her name and still have her initials spell bad." There was love and laughter in his voice. "She'll be all right even if some of her dreams don't become reality. That's part of growing up. She'd be more hurt if she thought you were avoiding her."

That made sense. All of my excuses and complications were falling away in my new reality. The one where I admitted how scared I was. And I was still afraid Daniel was wrong that his way was better. Wasn't it wrong to let him hang around hoping for something that wasn't going to happen? "I don't know," I said.

I heard Daniel exhale softly above me. His legs bent as he came down to sit in the grass, careful to keep Emmet between us. I noticed his respect for boundaries. "What don't you know?" he asked.

"I can't hurt anyone else. I promised myself, and I promised God. This feels dangerous."

"I wouldn't want you to break any promises so I guess you're stuck with me." Daniel was trying not to smile. Even in the midst of a serious moment, he had infectious joy.

"Why am I stuck with you?"

He cocked his head sideways as though the answer was obvious. "If you said you're not allowed to hurt *anyone*, that has to include you. All this nonsense about having to stay away from me because I'm in love with you is tearing you up. So just stop it."

I had turned away to see what Piper was up to on the field, and I froze in that direction. He loved me? He sounded more certain, not less, that he loved me. And he said it like it was the easiest thing in the world to stop worrying about hurting him. I took a moment to close my gaping mouth. When I turned to tell him I didn't know how to do that, he threw a handful of grass at me.

"I said stop it." He raised an eyebrow and began to pluck more ammunition. Daniel wasn't going to let me argue anymore.

The grass surprised the fight out of me. I finally caught the mood he was trying to spread and no longer wanted to argue. All I wanted was to enjoy the friendship. That and to get Emmet on my side in the ensuing grass fight.

# 15

Mom impressed me at the funeral home Friday evening. Person after person came up to talk to her, many of whom apologized for not visiting Dad more often in the last year or two. She said she knew how busy they were or acted as though she didn't realize it had been so long. She set the tone, which was somber but still allowed for occasional smiles as we greeted familiar faces or heard nice things about Dad.

My brother didn't make it. We shared a video chat earlier in the day though. It had been evening for him. His little girl got in front of the camera and said nothing. She just stared at us on the screen with wide, adorable eyes. Mom loved it.

Marie was at the funeral home with her husband David. I still felt as though I barely knew him, but the three of us talked like we were family. David was wearing a normal suit. Not that he ever wore anything weird. Suspenders were sort of unusual, I thought, for someone his age. It occurred to me that he could be wearing them under his jacket and I wouldn't know.

Marie happily talked about how her clothes were all getting tight. She didn't look obviously pregnant to me yet, but I wasn't about to burst her bubble. They moved on to chat with some extended family just as I got a phone call. It was my friend Audrey. She was the only person I had personally called to tell about losing my dad. She apologized for not being able to come in person and hoped it wasn't rude to call during the visitation.

I didn't know about the etiquette of the situation. I only knew she'd caught me alone and it was nice to hear from her. To continue the good timing, Daniel walked into the room as I hung up.

We had talked for the rest of soccer practice. When we were all tired of tossing grass – and the disapproving look I got from a nearby mom helped – we lay in the grass and tried to get Emmet to see interesting shapes in the clouds. The little boy had insisted they were all shaped like clouds and nothing else.

I left the field convinced we could actually choose to keep the relationship as it had been. Maybe forever. Maybe only indefinitely. Maybe I shouldn't have felt so grateful to Daniel for refusing to let me push him away.

I felt another surge of gratitude when I saw him enter the funeral home though. He straightened his tie, which actually made it more crooked, then began to scan the room. I knew he was looking for me. Despite what I thought was a head start on my grieving, my legs shifted to wobbly when his eyes locked on mine. It was as though I was suddenly allowed to feel off-balance now that I had someone to lean on.

I saw his mouth form the word hi before he quite reached me.

"Hi," I said.

"You look very nice tonight. I like that dress."

It was gray, bland and appropriate for the occasion. I'd also just worn it to church a couple weeks earlier. I supposed that starting with niceties was appropriate, too. "Thank you," I said. "And thanks for coming."

He glanced to an empty place beside him. "Brooke's with my mom tonight. I'm bringing her tomorrow. We were lucky to have the girls' team scheduled for the first two games. I think they can play and still get cleaned up before eleven o'clock. Though Brooke, and the coach, knows that we might have to leave early. I told her we'd try to sit by Piper at church and that made it okay."

I tried to smile as though I understood. I wanted to ask Daniel to sit with me instead. I couldn't do that because it might send a signal to that hope he was carrying. I swallowed the impulse, stuffing it in place next to the guilty part of me that didn't mind the hope.

"How's your mom doing?" he asked.

We both turned to look at her in the midst of a nearby crowd. Her hair was pinned up as sleek as ever, and she looked genuinely pleased to see the person she was greeting. "Better," I said to Daniel. "The first day, I... she just seemed more shocked than I expected given the circumstances. We talked about Dad today. We spent over an hour reminiscing. It made me realize that it'd been a long time since we'd talked about the good times." I paused to include a shrug. "I don't really know what that means or why it was easier now, but... it was nice."

Daniel seemed to understand what I was trying to say. I was going to tell him one of the stories about my dad. I got distracted by a large man I saw over his shoulder. I never thought of Daniel as a small man, though he was only an inch or two taller than me. The man who had materialized at his elbow was nearly a head taller and very broad. Daniel appeared small only by the contrast.

"Aaron?" I said. "Um... hi."

"Hi, Molly." He glanced between me and Daniel, asking with his eyes if he was interrupting anything.

Introductions seemed like my clearest option. "This is my friend Daniel. I knew Aaron at school."

There was an awkward pause while the guys silently shook hands. I think all three of us were registering the fact that I didn't say how well I knew Aaron.

Daniel began to slip away. "Maddie and Stephen are here. I'll just go say hello to them."

I nodded at him and looked at Aaron. "I guess you can tell I'm surprised to see you. How did you know about my dad?"

"Audrey posted something about it."

That made sense. Audrey and the guy she'd recently married were how I'd met Aaron in the first place. "And you drove all the way over here? I mean, thank you, but..."

"It's only three hours or so and I've never been to Thompsonville. I had an early dinner at this place called The Sleepy Crab. Do you know it?"

"Yeah. I was there recently."

"There's a big anchor out front and boat pictures, but it's not a seafood place. That's so awesome."

"Glad you liked it," I said. "How long are you in town?"

"Just today. I'm driving back after this."

"Oh. That's quick."

"Yeah. Sorry I won't make it to the funeral. I thought tonight would be a better chance to talk anyway. I wanted…" Aaron looked around and took a small step closer to me. "I wanted to tell you that I regret the way we left things. Two years and I still hate myself when… I should not have said some of the things I said and being upset was no excuse."

"I think you had a right to be upset."

He tilted his head to acknowledge my comment and said, "It still doesn't… I was awful to you. I hope we can forgive each other?"

I wanted to tell him there was nothing to forgive because I was sure my side was much worse. But I heard in his olive branch that I was forgiven. It meant so much to me that I had to offer anything I could. "Yes," I said. "I know you didn't mean it."

He nodded and reached out to give me a quick hug. We said our goodbyes, and I watched him leave. I hadn't spoken to Aaron since we broke up. I barely thought about him except to wish we'd never met because the end was so painful. Maybe now I'd be able to remember that we'd had a little fun, too.

"Hey, you okay?" Daniel was back, a touch of concern on his face.

"I'm fine," I said. "Really." I smiled to convince him. "That was surprising but not bad. Hi, Marie." My sister had followed Daniel and her husband was just behind her. "Have you met my sister?"

"Yeah." Marie answered for him. "We came to Sacred Heart for Easter, remember?"

"Oh, that's right."

"Good to see you again, Daniel."

"Same to you," he said, "though I'm sorry about the circumstances."

She acknowledged the sympathy, then looked at me and said, "So I actually came over here for a reason. I was just talking to Mom, and she said she didn't know what she was going to do with all the time she's been spending at Creekside. I don't know about most of it, but I wondered if maybe Sundays you and Mom could start coming out to the farm for lunch."

"*Every* Sunday?"

"Yes." She looked to David, who nodded his confirmation. "We've been wanting to try to start up some regular family time, but it felt… wrong somehow to do something that Dad couldn't come to."

It seemed that several things had been put on hold while we waited for Dad to pass. "I think that'd be great. You wouldn't mind hosting all the time?"

"No, no. It'll be easier on us, especially when the little one joins us." Marie patted her belly and tried to emphasize the curve that wasn't all that curvy. "And Daniel, you and Brooke should come, too. Do you have any Sunday afternoon obligations?"

"I… uh… I don't." He stumbled over the words in surprise then looked at me for help. He knew that including him in the family gathering implied something I didn't want to imply. My tongue locked up. I wanted him to come no matter what it implied to others. It would be so wonderful if he came. But I was supposed to be putting up with hope, not encouraging it. Why was keeping this relationship simple the most complicated thing I'd ever done?

****

A few people stopped by the house after the funeral on Saturday. They stayed only long enough to leave food for us. Marie and David went straight back to their farm. Mom and I had a quiet afternoon. Mom would normally have spent some time at Creekside, and I usually found some chores or errands to do. I didn't want to look back in twenty years and know that I did laundry or something else mundane on the day my dad was buried. It may have been a strange feeling, but it wasn't one I could help.

For the most part, I anxiously paced the house or wandered inside my head, not really thinking about much of anything. Mom put her music on before dinner. I took that to mean that she noticed how quiet the house was, too. She left the volume soft so I took a seat and asked if she wanted to talk about something.

She rather shocked me when she said, "Would you be upset if I started dating?"

"I, uh... when... uh, what do you mean?"

"I don't have anyone in particular in mind." Mom was amused by my tripping over an answer. I got the feeling she'd been mischievous on purpose. "I also don't mean tomorrow or even soon. I've been thinking of taking up a new hobby so I don't spend all the time I used to spend visiting your dad thinking about how I used to spend that time visiting your dad. And I think I might like to take an art class."

"Interesting," I said. Art sounded messy to me. While I'd immediately changed into comfy shorts after the funeral, Mom was still in her nice clothes. I looked at her black skirt and crisply ironed blouse and had a hard time picturing her doing anything messy. "But what does art class have to do with you dating?"

"Maybe nothing." She shrugged. "I just thought I might make a friend. And what if that friend is a gentleman? And what if..." She shrugged again. "I wondered what you and your complication avoidance would think of that?"

"Not *every* man is a complication, Mom."

"Really?" She lifted her eyebrows and gave me the feeling we were going to keep talking about me.

I was saved by the bell, so to speak. My phone requested attention. "It's Audrey," I said as I answered.

"Molly, hi."

"Hey. What's up?"

"I have a favor to ask of you."

"Okay," I said. "What is it?"

"Well, you know how I like to play matchmaker?"

"Oh, dear. You haven't given that up?" I tried to put teasing into my tone and not the dread I actually felt.

"Never," Audrey said, laughing. "There's this guy I work with and he... I think you might like him. Don't worry about the distance. He's willing to drive to Thompsonville."

Wow. Audrey found a guy willing to drive three hours for a blind date. She could spin that as pathetic and desperate or just plain determined. It didn't matter since I wasn't interested either way. "I appreciate the suggestion, but I really don't think this is a good time for me. With my dad and all."

"Yeah?" I could hear her disappointment. "I thought maybe a new guy could cheer you up."

"I'm sorry. I think he's going to have to cheer up someone else."

"All right. Promise it'll be less than a year before we talk again?"

"Of course." I hung up laughing and promising myself I'd be better at keeping in touch with Audrey.

Mom bumped her brows up to question me.

"Audrey still thinks she's a matchmaker," I said.

"And you're not interested because of Daniel?"

"No, Mom," I said, with a little too much impatience. "I'm not interested because long distance relationships are complicated and this doesn't feel like a good time to bring someone new into my life and I'm not excited about a blind date in general and..." There were probably a lot of other reasons I couldn't think of at the moment. None of them had anything to do with the man who was hoping for something that couldn't happen.

"Just tell me one thing." Mom gave me a serious but soft look. "When Audrey mentioned fixing you up, were you thinking about Daniel?"

I was. I knew I was. When she said a guy could cheer me up, I thought that one already had. But I didn't think of him because he was a guy. I thought of him because he was a friend. He just happened to be the first friend I thought of. Every single time.

Mom said, "I saw you talking to Aaron last night."

Finally, we could talk about something else. "Yeah. He drove all the way here to say he was sorry about the way we ended things." Then I quickly added, "And because he'd never been to Thompsonville."

Mom snickered. She understood how exhausting I thought his adventures were.

"Still," I said, "it was sweet. You know how sometimes you don't know you need something until you have it?"

"Like closure or something?"

I nodded.

"Forgiveness?" Mom said.

I nodded again.

"Molly, don't you think it's time you forgive yourself?"

"I don't—"

She refused to hear my protest. "I know you feel bad that people have gotten hurt, and that's a good reason to take things slowly and be cautious. But it's not a good reason for keeping at arm's length a man who's completely nuts about you, not when you're also nuts about him."

No rebuttal came to mind. No words could capture my confusion. What she said actually sounded reasonable, but it didn't *feel* reasonable. I could not shake the idea that there was something wrong with the picture of me and Daniel together.

"I'm just going to say one more motherly thing, and then I promise I'll butt out altogether." She paused to make sure I was listening. "The longer you punish yourself, the longer you punish Daniel. And I don't think that's what you want to do."

She ended the discussion by turning up the song playing in the background. The notes I usually tuned out seemed to swell with the strength of her argument. Was it true? Was I limiting my relationship with Daniel because I was punishing myself? Did I think I deserved to be hurt because of the pain I'd caused? Daniel wasn't going to hurt me. Was I really scared not because I wasn't supposed to love him, but because he wasn't supposed to love me back?

# 16

I was still pondering some serious questions in church the next morning. Mistakes and intent. Daniel. Regret and forgiveness. Daniel. Past and future. Daniel. What I wanted and what I was worthy of. Church was a good place for questioning, but I didn't feel any answers. I went through the motions of prayer and song. I knew there was grace there. I could not find it. I tried to empty myself, to be ready when clarity found me.

I watched the congregation filing from the building. I watched my mom moving from her place in the choir. I sighed and headed for the parish hall myself. Perhaps a donut would prove to be just what I needed. There was typically a one-way flow of people into the hall for coffee and donuts. But something was different that morning. People were going in *and* out, confused looks and shrugged shoulders everywhere. In the midst of all the movement, I saw one person standing completely still.

It was as though God used the contrast to point Daniel out to me with a giant invisible arrow. It felt like healing and permission to move on. I couldn't undo past suffering by imposing some on myself. I was through trying. For what felt like the tenth time in as many days, I had to admit Mom was right. It was time to forgive myself. It was time to stop pretending there was anything complicated about how I felt when I looked at Daniel. I was happy. I did deserve to love him. Not because I never meant to hurt James, not because Aaron had forgiven me, and certainly not because I'd never make another mistake. I deserved love because I was a child of God. And so was Daniel.

He was standing by the playground. I moved through the crowd to get to him. "Good morning," I said. "Is something going on back there?"

Daniel smiled and shook his head at the same time. "Apparently, it was Stephen's turn to pick up the donuts this morning and he told Maddie someone else had volunteered without mentioning that the someone else was her brother."

"Tim?"

"Yeah. I guess he's notoriously unreliable. The donuts are not here yet and when Maddie found out Stephen let Tim get them, she asked me to take the kids outside so she could handle the situation." Daniel winced. "I'm afraid 'handle the situation' might be code for giving Stephen an earful. She was already laying into him before we got out."

"I see," I said. "Do you mind if I stay out here with you then?"

"Of course not." He offered a playful grin and said, "Race you to the swings?"

I snorted as though I thought he was kidding. Then I sprinted towards the swings. It was probably not very ladylike to run in a dress, but the closest swing wasn't more than twenty feet away. The short distance and cheap head start let me get there first. I grabbed the chain and sat down. Daniel laughed as he moved past me to take the next swing.

"I won," I said. "That means you have to push me."

He let go of the other swing and went behind me instead. He put his hand, a very warm hand, in the middle of my back and let out a fake groan. "I don't think I can."

"You better be careful, mister," I said. "Some women would not appreciate a crack about their weight." I saw Emmet coming over to join us.

"That wasn't a crack about your weight," Daniel said. "It was a crack about my lack of strength."

I thought Emmet was going to take the next swing, but he got between me and Daniel instead. "I'll help you," he said. I felt two much smaller hands on my lower back. It felt as though they were exerting true effort and still not moving me.

"I don't think this is going to work." Daniel stepped back. "Emmet, how about you take this other swing. I'll push you, and we'll make Molly push herself."

"Okay." Emmet was agreeable, but he needed help getting onto the swing. They were high for a preschool playground, which was the reason I wasn't eating my knees as I rocked back and forth with my feet on the ground. Emmet got a good ride while I mostly relaxed.

Piper and Brooke were giggling under the slide and appeared to be ducking away from imaginary attackers. A powerful smile came over me that almost had me laughing with them. It felt so good to let everything go. I knew my dad was in a better place. I still missed him, would always miss him, but I no longer felt guilty for missing him now that he was fully gone. I was beginning to let myself imagine a future with Daniel, possibly one that had our kids giggling under a slide.

I always knew that God forgives us. It was in so many verses and Sunday school lessons and homilies and yet I hadn't let it apply to me. I'd asked to be forgiven over and over without accepting that forgiveness when it came. I finally felt peace and contentment. I'd need to find a time to let Daniel know that I also felt love.

"Kids!" Maddie's voice announced her arrival at the playground gate. "Uncle Tim finally showed up. We're going to grab a few donuts and take them home to eat." After confirming that her little ones were moving in her direction, she added, "Bye, Molly. Bye, Daniel."

We waved to her and Daniel took the swing Emmet had jumped from as Brooke ran towards us. "Are we gonna have a donut, too, Dad?"

"Hmmm… I don't know." Daniel sighed as though he was suffering over the question. "I just sat down and if we're going to have lunch with Molly's sister, we probably shouldn't spoil our appetites."

Brooke flicked a braid over her shoulder as she cocked her head to the side. "Just say yes or no, Dad."

He smiled and said. "No, then."

Surprise flashed on Brooke's face before she nodded curtly and turned away.

She'd only made it a few steps before Daniel said, "All right. Let's go in and see if we can find small donuts."

Brooke lit up so much she skipped towards the gate.

"You coming?" Daniel offered me a hand from the swing.

"Yeah." He let go as soon as I was standing. I felt the loss, but I had set the limits and trying to hang on before we talked would only cause additional confusion. "I'll see when my mom'll be ready to go."

Daniel opened his mouth to respond, but I cut him off.

"But I'll still sit with you and Brooke."

"I'm glad you've come to your senses there, but, uh…" He smiled only faintly. "Well, I know your sister backed you into a corner about extending the invitation for today. If you want to make excuses to her, I can come up with something to tell Brooke."

"No, I don't need to make excuses."

"You sure?"

I looked into familiar eyes with a still unfamiliar, but welcome, certainty. "I'm sure," I said.

"You could tell her I've come down with bubonic plague." Daniel gave me a cheeky grin. He apparently doubted my certainty.

"Stop it," I said, giving his arm a gentle shove. "It's just lunch. I'm not worried about… And you know Brooke will like the animals."

"And you want me to come." Daniel still looked playful as he said, "It'd be nice if you admitted it."

I had too much to admit in the two seconds it would take us to enter the building. We walked into the air conditioning of the parish hall. It was about half as full as usual. Monsignor Loy greeted us. "Welcome," he said. "Help us out so none of those delicious donuts go to waste."

"If you insist," Daniel said.

The priest gave a jovial laugh as he moved on.

"If you admit you were going to have a donut anyway, I'll admit I want you to come to Marie and David's with us."

Daniel squinted in confusion. "Is that supposed to be a fair trade? You know I'm a fan of donuts." He pulled a few dollars from his pocket as he talked and deposited them into the coffee and donut fund.

"Depends what you mean by fair."

"What do you mean by that?" He still looked confused, but also like he was enjoying the confusion.

I smiled, too. "Maybe I feel like being mysterious today."

"Or just frustrating." Daniel reached into the box and picked up a donut. "I noticed you haven't actually admitted anything."

"Admitted what?" Brooke was standing between us holding a donut that was already half-eaten. Some of it was in her mouth as she talked.

"Your dad wants me to admit I'm happy even though I'm smiling," I said. "Weird, huh?"

She shrugged in a way that implied she thought we were both weird.

Daniel said, "You do look unusually happy today." The thought seemed to please him.

"Come on," I said. "We can all go see if my mom is ready to go."

I led the way to my mom's table and just assumed the others would follow me. She caught my eye as I approached, and I could hear her bidding the others a good day. The woman next to her was Maddie's mom. Then I realized that the man next to her was Tim. Maddie's mom was also his mom so it made sense for him to be there. I sent a nervous glance over my shoulder. Daniel and Brooke were right on my heels. What were the odds that something awkward was about to happen?

Mom stood up right away. I tried to offer a friendly greeting to the table as a whole. "Sorry to steal her away," I said.

"No problem, Molly," Maddie's mom said. I could not remember her name at the moment. "We're all sorry about your dad."

"Thank you," I said.

There was a bit of sympathetic nodding. Mom stepped away from the table, and I thought we were about to make a clean getaway.

Then Tim spoke up, right in front of everyone. "So I was late with the donuts today and Maddie said I could make up for that by asking you out again, but I thought you made it clear that wasn't going to happen. Should I ignore my sister on this one?" He was looking at me as were lots of other eyes.

I bit my lip hard as I figured out how to answer tactfully. Perhaps it was safest to simply agree with him. "I... I think you can safely ignore your sister on this one."

He nodded and stuffed a huge chunk of donut into his mouth.

I turned away and nearly ran into Daniel. "Did he say again?"

"We had dinner a week or so ago," I said. "It wasn't a big deal."

"Was that before or after—" Daniel stopped abruptly. He absorbed the fact that his daughter and my mom were among the people staring at us.

I knew what he wanted to ask. How could I have had a date with someone else while keeping that option so firmly off the table between us? How could I think about anyone else after the way I'd kissed him? Now that I understood my own mind, I could explain it to Daniel. But this was not the right time or the right place. "I promise we'll find time to talk this afternoon," I said.

He closed his eyes as he nodded.

"Okay," Mom said. "Let's get this show on the road."

Brooke rode with us as we followed Daniel to his house to drop off his car, then he climbed into the backseat with his daughter. The hour drive felt much shorter as we talked and laughed and had friendly arguments over which songs on the radio were worth a listen.

There was a small house almost directly across the street and otherwise no neighbors in sight of my sister's house. They had a large barn, what looked like a shed but I knew was a coop, and a strong smell of animals in the air. Brooke complained about the smell and I told her she wouldn't notice it after we'd been there a while. She did not seem to find that reassuring.

Marie greeted us at the door. It had only been two days since I decided she didn't look pregnant. Something about the way the waistband of her dress was pushed up made me think her stomach had grown in those two days. She'd waited so long to tell us that we were barely five months from a new addition to the family. That small rounded belly filled me with more excitement about the prospect than I'd felt so far. I reached out for a quick hug, though I wasn't normally much of a hugger.

"Welcome, everyone," Marie said. "Come on in."

The outdoor smells were quickly replaced by the wonderful aroma of fresh bread as we crossed the threshold.

"Excuse the mess," Marie said as she waved her arm towards the main room of the first floor. There was a couch on one side and a worktable filling most of the room. It was covered with thread and cloth. "I've just started trying to make some baby clothes, and I'm afraid I nearly had a tantrum of my own trying to figure it out yesterday."

"Well..." Mom looked thoroughly smug. "It's not as though anyone tried to teach you to sew when you were younger."

"I know, Mom." Marie put on a contrite face. "If I admit that I now wish I'd been a more willing student, will you help me?"

Mom smiled and hurried over to check out the fabric. "Of course, honey."

Brooke seemed intrigued by the mess. "Can I sew something, too?" she asked.

"Two willing students!" Mom took a seat and waved Brooke and Marie to either side of her.

I found a place for myself, though I thought I might only watch. I had let Mom teach me some basics. It was doubtful I'd remember much of the skills I hadn't used in ten years.

Marie looked up at Daniel. "David is somewhere in the field. You're welcome to look for him if wandering the farm sounds more appealing than being sucked into a sewing circle. Lunch is at least a half hour from being ready."

He looked to me for input.

I just smiled and shrugged. I kind of wanted him to stick around, but I figured he'd rather hunt down a little more testosterone.

Then he looked at Brooke.

She not-so-subtly gestured for him to leave the room.

"All right," he said with a laugh. "I know when I'm not wanted."

The front door had barely closed behind Daniel when Marie wiggled her eyebrows at me and said, "So when's the wedding?" Her suggestion that Daniel would rather be somewhere else lost its altruistic glow.

This definitely felt like a family gathering. I wasn't sure this was a subject we should discuss in front of Brooke though.

Brooke appeared to sense the reason for my hesitation. "It's okay," she said. "Piper already told me that you said you'd marry my dad if he asked you."

"That's not what I said." Sometimes kids really did have their own reality. I didn't know if this was Brooke's or Piper's. Either way, my defensive statement caused sadness. Brooke looked down as though I'd yelled at her.

Marie and my mom were still looking at me as though I needed to answer the first question.

"Piper was concerned that if I got married, I couldn't be her nanny anymore. I told her I could do both, but we were talking about possibilities not... not anything actually being planned."

Brooke sort of nodded but still looked chastised.

"So it is a possibility?" Mom said. It didn't appear she or Marie were going to let me off with a hypothetical.

"As far as me and Daniel are concerned, or me and your dad," I said, "can we just say that no one is planning a wedding *right now* and leave it at that?"

Mom smiled. I think she understood that she'd gotten through to me. I was saying I was no longer avoiding that possibility, and she heard that.

Marie also seemed pleased with the prospect.

Brooke said, "*When* are you getting married?"

"I don't know," I said. "If, you hear me saying if, right?" She nodded.

"*If* we ever start planning a wedding, I promise you can be the first to know."

"Okay," she said. She smiled and turned excitedly to my mom. "Can we make a dress for me to wear to the wedding?"

Perhaps she didn't hear the if after all.

# 17

Lunch was fabulous. Marie simply made soup and bread. But the bread was still warm from the oven, and the soup was perfectly seasoned. She believed she was behind on her sewing skills. Her cooking, however, didn't leave any room for improvement.

I found myself watching Daniel during the meal. He was sitting right across from me. My eyes felt strangely shy though. They jumped away whenever he looked in my direction. I think I was afraid he'd read my change in thoughts before I had a chance to tell him. I was looking forward to a private conversation. Brooke asked if we could return to the sewing lesson after we finished eating.

The men volunteered to clean up the kitchen. Daniel and David sat on the other side of the room when they were done. They seemed to be getting along. After a while, Brooke's attention seemed to be shifting to that side of the room as she lost interest in the project. At least for the moment. When she asked if they were talking about animals, David said, "Your dad says you might like to meet Sally."

"Is that your cow?"

"Yes," Marie said. "We have chickens, too."

Brooke's eyes widened. "Can I see?"

"Sure." Marie waved at the cloth Brooke was holding. "Just leave that right there."

David rose to lead the tour and took hold of Marie's hand as they moved to the back door.

My mom followed Brooke. She looked back at me as I was the last to move to leave. "You've seen the animals before, haven't you?" she said, sending her eyes quickly over her shoulder to Daniel, then back.

Daniel said, "Now who's not wanted?"

"Fine," I said, sitting myself back down, "I'll stay here and sew that sleeve inside out for you."

"Fine." Mom winked at me. "As long as Daniel helps."

Daniel stopped at the doorway. He wore an expression of mild surprise as my mom walked past him. Then he smiled at something she said and came towards me. "She said I'm wanted in here."

"I wonder what she meant by that." I tried to act coy because while I did want to talk to Daniel alone, having my mom arrange it for me wasn't what I had in mind.

He stepped forward to the table of sewing projects. He said nothing as he surveyed the work. There was disappointment in the silence before he said, "I don't think I can be much help here."

"Daniel," I said, "I need to apologize to you."

"For going out with Maddie's brother?"

My turn to be surprised. I didn't want to talk about Tim. I already said that wasn't a big deal. Had Daniel been thinking about him since we saw him at church?

"You don't have to apologize," he said. "You're the one who's been clear about where I stand. I can't be upset."

Even though Daniel said he couldn't be upset, I could see and hear that he was. That hurt me. "Then let me explain. The only reason I went out with Tim is because I was trying to prove to myself that there was nothing going on between us and you know what… it was awful. I spent the whole time trying not to wish he was you."

"I don't want to talk about anyone else."

"Neither do I. You're the one who brought him up."

"I didn't—" Daniel looked confused for a moment, until he cut himself off with a dismissive eye roll. He picked up a spool of thread to redirect the conversation. "Do you think Brooke could take something home in case she wants to make some more progress? Or would it be better to leave it here to keep her interest up for next week?"

"Whatever you think is best. Mom would probably love to help her if she got to the next step before Sunday."

He nodded and set the thread back down. I didn't think he really wanted to talk about sewing either. "Should we catch up to the others?"

"Not yet," I said. "You didn't let me apologize for what I actually wanted to apologize for."

"Oh. What did you do?"

"I... I've been incredibly obtuse."

He stared at me for a moment before the corners of his mouth began to twitch as he fought a laugh. He put his hand over his mouth and looked up in a plea for help.

I got it. That apology made no sense. I'd probably laugh if someone apologized for being obtuse and expected me not to appear the same. I stood up and walked around the table to be closer and make a better attempt to clarify my position.

Daniel stopped the battle and became naturally serious with my proximity. Perhaps my body language was already speaking for me.

"What I mean is... I've been unfair to you and the fact that I didn't mean to is no excuse. It clearly looked like I wanted to, uh, change the rules with you and then I didn't and then... I just didn't think I deserved you. And now I know I don't, but I no longer care."

"Keep talking," Daniel said. "I think you're telling me something good, but you're kind of babbling and I don't want to be the one who's obtuse."

I needed to be clearer. "I've been saying that I don't want to get involved unless I could be sure that... but I'm already involved, like head over heels involved." I needed to be absolutely clear. "I love you and I'm ready to... change the rules."

"Okay." He wrapped his arms around me in a tight hug and whispered, "I love you, too," in my ear.

It felt like heaven, to love and be loved, to know this man making my heart race was someone I could trust. But it also felt almost too easy to believe. "Just like that?" I said into his shoulder. "You don't even want to give me a hard time about jerking you around?"

His head shook next to mine. Then he pulled back enough to look at me and said, "Just like that. And this." I watched his eyes travel down to my mouth before he kissed me. He moved slowly but with no hesitation.

I practiced a little more restraint, and I knew it was because I wasn't thinking it might be my only chance. It was a very tender kiss. Daniel looked at me afterwards and something wicked sparked in his eyes. "Since you offered though, I'd like to reserve the right to give you a hard time about it at some point in the future."

"That's not how it works."

"Are you sure?"

With his hands still on my waist, I wasn't sure of much.

"You said we were going to change the rules. I vote for that one. From now on, I get to hold this over your head whenever you try to accuse *me* of being difficult."

I just shook my head because he was already being difficult, trying to get a rise out of me.

"No? What did you mean when you said change the rules?"

My emotions were precariously close to overwhelming me. It was a good kind of overwhelmed, but I didn't want to get carried away. Better to try to match his playful mood. "I don't think we have enough time to list all the rules right now. You'll have to make an appointment so we can discuss it later."

He came close enough that I felt the laugh rumble in his chest before his hand stroked the back of my head. "I think I'll need a lot of appointments." Then he inhaled strongly, apparently bracing himself, as he stepped back and left only our hands together. "Can I make one serious request though?"

I nodded.

"Can we not... maybe not tell anyone until we're ready for a real announcement?"

"I am very okay with insisting to everyone else that we're just friends until, well, until Brooke is designing the invitations."

Daniel laughed and took something from his pocket. He unfolded the paper and handed it to me.

It was a hand drawn wedding invitation. There was a smiling couple on the front labeled Molly and Dad. The invitation promised yummy cake and listed Piper and Brooke as bridesmaids. The only missing detail was a blank line next to the word date. "Brooke made that yesterday. You might need to pick another condition," Daniel said.

"I guess until you're ready to…" My words trailed off because I was pointing to that blank line and saw Daniel shaking his head out of the corner of my eye. That wasn't giving us time either? Oh, boy. Daniel had been more patient with me than I realized. I slowly folded the paper and slipped it into my pocket.

"How about I'll hold on to this," I said, "and we can tell people when looking at it doesn't turn my legs to jelly?"

"I can live with that," he said. "Anything that makes them guess when you stopped resisting my charms. No one would believe how long you held out anyway."

"Least of all me." I was serious and also laughing. "Ready to follow everyone to the barn now? I'm sure they're already speculating, but it'll get worse the longer we're in here."

He leaned in to kiss me one more time first. Then we held hands only until we got to the back door. We slipped into the back of the group while Marie was showing Brooke how she checks for eggs. Daniel quietly moved closer to his daughter, who I'm pretty sure hadn't noticed we were missing.

My mom, however, patted my shoulder and said, "Can I be the second to know?"

I smiled at what we both already knew. There was no point in pretending otherwise. That would only complicate matters.

## Stories From Hartford series

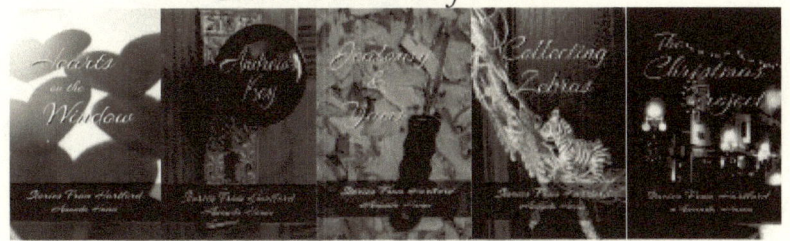

## Coffee and Donuts series

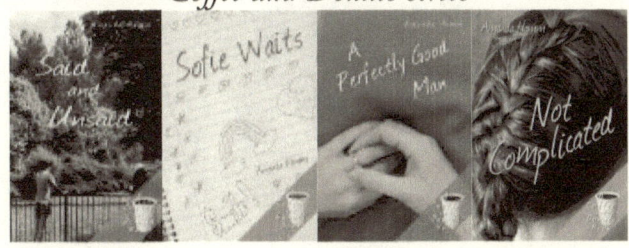

## More titles